THE DEFIANT

AN UNBEATEN PATH

BOOK TWO
THE DEFIANT SERIES

D1503786

JOHN W. VANCE

Copyright © 2015 John W. Vance
No part of this book may be reproduced in any manner
whatsoever without permission except in the case of brief
quotations embodied in critical articles or reviews.
For information contact:
info@jwvance.com
www.jwvance.com
All rights reserved.
ISBN: 10: 1514106477
ISBN-13: 978-1514106471

DEDICATION

TO THOSE WHO KEEP THE WOLVES AT BAY

ACKNOWLEDGMENTS

I need to acknowledge my wife and my young family. You are my inspiration and the force that drives me to be a better man each and every day. If my life was not graced with your presence I'd be lost in this world. Not a day goes by where I don't look at your faces and cherish my life with you all.

Thank you for your support, encouragement and critique. It is priceless.

Love – John (aka Daddy)

PROLOGUE

Outside Oklahoma City, Texas Federation
Not Too Distant Future

Abigail paced the wood floors of the kitchen. The sun hadn't yet graced the windows of her home, but soon would. Sleep had been impossible for her. All night she'd tossed and turned from the anticipation of answering questions she didn't really want to answer.

It was natural for Alexis to want to know where she came from and who her father really was. She just hated that it was thrust on her at a time she didn't choose. She had always planned on telling her, but as Alexis grew, it became more and more acceptable in her mind to put it off. Year after year she would rationalize a reason for not telling her, but deep down she knew she was making a mistake by not being honest with her. When pressed by her late husband's brother, Phillip, to come clean with Alexis, she refused, citing that Alexis needed to be protected. His question was, "Protecting her from what?" It was a question she couldn't really answer.

Abigail at first didn't want Alexis to grow up thinking she had been abandoned, and with Samuel around, why confuse her. For all intents and purposes, Samuel was her father, daddy, dad, papa, etc. He was all of it for her and she knew no different. Telling her at a very young age would only confuse her, she had thought. But when Alexis turned thirteen, Abigail had thought about sitting her down and confessing, but she again thought it might confuse her.

It had taken Alexis a long time to come to grips with losing Samuel, and just when she was coming to terms with his death, Abigail thought it not a good time to tell her about Luke and what happened to him. The last thing Abigail wanted for Alexis was to feel she had lost two fathers.

All of it was confusing and no time ever seemed right, but regardless of all of her past refusals to tell her, it came up. Now she wanted to control just what information Alexis heard. However, that would be hard, as Phillip thought it best to tell children everything so that they be better prepared. While Abigail tried to protect Alexis, Phillip's view was that a child shouldn't be coddled. She didn't do that with Alexis, but her instincts were to ensure she was shielded against unnecessary emotional burdens.

Abigail paused and looked out the window. The orange dawn glow lit the morning clouds and began to cast its light upon the rolling fields. She looked at her garden and the land she called home beyond it. This was her home and she loved it. Besides his deep love and affection, her house and rich land was one of Samuel's greatest gifts to her. Samuel and Alexis had turned that house into a home and she would forever be grateful. She had several men to thank for her blessings in life, her father, Samuel and Luke. Sadly all three were gone, taken away when the storm clouds of a long civil war came.

"Why didn't you ever tell me?" Alexis blurted out from

the doorway of the kitchen.

The question jolted Abigail and brought her back to the present. She turned and smiled at Alexis. "Good morning, sweetie."

Alexis sauntered in the kitchen and sat at a small circular table. She picked a tomato from the bowl that sat in the center and began to roll it from one hand to the next. "So why hide it from me?"

Abigail sighed and quickly took a seat at the table. She reached over and took one of Alexis' hands. With a firm grip she again sighed. Her eyes welled up with tears as she fought to find the *right* answer.

"I just don't understand why you weren't honest with me," Alexis lamented.

"Oh, sweetie, I didn't do it to hurt you, you must believe that."

"I know that, Mom, I just want to know everything. Can we start now?"

"I'll tell you more, but how about we have some breakfast first," Abigail said.

"That's not what I meant."

Abigail furrowed her brow.

"Can we start being completely honest with each other, about everything? You know the world better than I do. I'm not a child anymore and I think we need to be honest."

Abigail tightened her grip and smiled. "How did you become so wise?"

"I don't know where. Where did I?"

"It wasn't your father, I mean your biological father, and it definitely wasn't me, so I'll have to say it came from your grandparents."

"I wish I could have met them."

"You did, you just don't remember them," Abigail said, looking down; a deep emotional pain crept into her expression.

"I'm sorry; I shouldn't have brought them up."

Abigail wiped away a few tears and said, "It's okay, it just makes me sad is all. If it wasn't for them, we wouldn't be here, but you know that already. I think I tell you almost daily."

"I like hearing it, makes me appreciate where I come from and just how fortunate I am."

"Starting right this second, I swear to you I'll never hold anything back. You're everything to me and all I thought I was doing was protecting you. I was wrong."

"How did you meet?"

"I owe that story to you, don't I?" Abigail said, admitting that the stories the day before never touched on Luke.

"Yes, you do owe me," Alexis joked.

"How about some breakfast first?"

"I'm not hungry and I think you're stalling."

Abigail smiled and wiped a few more tears from her eyes. Alexis was right; it was a stall tactic because she didn't know where to begin.

Alexis leaned in closer and whispered, "I'll be fine, Mom, with whatever you tell me. I'm a big girl now."

Abigail patted Alexis' hand and said, "I know you are, I know that. It's just I don't know how to begin."

"How to begin? Just start from the beginning. Don't

try to spin it, just tell me everything."

Abigail took a deep breath, exhaled and said, "The beginning it will be, then." Abigail hesitated because the first time she met Luke was a very violent tragic day. For several years she thought it a chance encounter, but as the years wore on and Alexis grew, she came to believe that their meeting wasn't chance but destiny.

"Mom?" Alexis pressed, seeing her mother drift deep in thought.

"Sorry, I'm trying to collect the memories."

The first rays of sunlight penetrated the clouds and streamed into the kitchen. One beam landed on their grasp and began to warm them. They both took notice and smiled.

"Look at that." Abigail laughed.

"I love you, Mom." Alexis smiled.

"I love you too, sweetheart," Abigail said, beaming with intense love for her beautiful daughter. She cleared her throat and said, "I met your father not a week after where I left off yesterday. That day is seared into my memory; it was horrible, truly horrible." Abigail paused and looked away.

"Please, Mom, don't hold back. I want to know everything."

"You won't like your father too much, so please have some context."

"Just be honest."

"I'm just worried you'll think him a bad man. He was just trying to survive in a world that was only beginning to fall apart."

"Mom, I'm not here to pass judgment. I just need to

know where I came from."

Abigail looked back at Alexis and said, "What happened that day would lead me to witness firsthand just how barbaric humans can be."

CHAPTER ONE

"If history repeats itself and the unexpected always happens, how incapable must Man be of learning from his experience." – George Bernard Shaw

U.S. Highway 91, six miles southwest of Wellsville, Utah

Colin slammed on the breaks, forcing the old Suburban to an immediate stop. All inside slammed against their seatbelts; those riding in the trailer they were towing weren't as prepared. The sudden and unexpected stop tossed them like rag dolls.

Nicolas, who had been napping in the front passenger seat, cried out, "What? What's going on?" His saucer-wide eyes spotted the reason, a teenage boy standing with his arms held high directly in the middle of the two-lane road.

The boy was frantic and wide eyed. He waved his arms back and forth and screamed out, "Stop, please! We need help!"

Colin looked over at Nicholas and asked in his deep Louisiana drawl, "What do you think, boss?"

Sitting behind Nicholas, Becky leaned up and said, "He looks scared."

"Try to go around him," Nicholas ordered.

Colin turned the wheel and slowly accelerated, but the

7

boy ran up to the Suburban and planted his bloody hands down on the hood. "Please help us!"

"Want me to run him over?" Colin asked.

Nicholas grunted and said, "I need eyes looking all around. This could be a trap."

"He looks genuinely terrified," Becky responded.

Nicholas scanned the area, but unfortunately there wasn't much to see. They were located near an S turn in the road with a rocky steep hill to their left and an equally steep drop-off to the right. Looking to his right, Nicholas saw the hill ended twenty feet into a thick forest of pine trees.

"Please help!" the boy cried out and slammed his hands into the hood again.

"Enough!" Nicholas fired back at him and opened his door.

"I'll cover you, boss," Colin offered.

"Becky, get behind the wheel, and, Colin, I told you, stop calling me boss."

Nicholas stepped away from the door and closed it. He slung his AR-15 and placed his hand on the back strap of his holstered Sig P239.

The boy turned to him and cried, "Please, you need to go help my sister!"

"Listen, I don't know who you are, but please step aside," Nicholas said, his left arm extended out in front of him just in case the boy rushed him. Now outside, Nicholas could see the boy's face was covered in blood and so was the front of his soiled clothes.

The boy stepped away from the front and took a step towards Nicholas.

"I wouldn't do that, son," Colin recommended.

The boy spun his head and cringed when he saw Colin's towering physique not five feet from him.

"I'm not here to hurt anyone; I just need someone to help my sister. She was attacked by some dogs. She's bleeding badly!"

Colin walked past the boy and stood next to the guard rail. He peered into the tree line below, looking for anything suspicious.

"So that's your sister's blood?" Nicholas asked.

"Yeah."

"Did you kill the dogs?" Nicholas asked.

Ignoring Nicholas, he replied, "She's close by. Please help me."

"What's this?" Bryn asked, walking up behind Nicholas.

"The boy jumped in front of the truck. I almost hit him," Colin answered.

"You should have," Bryn replied and continued, "Nic, this could be a trap. Look around, not a bad place to ambush us."

Not taking his eyes off the boy, Nicholas responded, "I realize this isn't the most ideal location to stop, but running him over wasn't prudent either."

"Hmm, let's hope you're right." Bryn smirked.

"Can you help me, please?" the boy asked.

"When did this happen?" Nicholas queried.

"About an hour ago. I saw the road and ran up; then I saw you coming," the boy replied.

"What was her condition when you left her?" Nicholas

said.

"She was alive, but she's been badly hurt."

Bryn looked at him suspiciously and tapped Nicholas on the shoulder.

Nicholas leaned back.

"I don't trust this fucking kid. Something's off about the whole thing," Bryn whispered.

Nicholas nodded and asked the boy, "How did you come to be attacked by dogs?"

"I don't know, we were hiking and they came upon us."

"What kind of dogs?" Nicholas pressed.

"Um, I don't know, big dogs, probably pit bulls," the boy answered.

"It's funny that every bad dog nowadays is a pit bull," Bryn snarled.

"Nic, we need to help," Becky said from behind the steering wheel.

"Please help. She's not that far and she needs me," the boy replied and pointed towards the trees to the right of them.

"Nic, we're a day's drive from the ranch. This isn't a good idea," Bryn blurted out.

"Please, she needs your help. She'll die if she doesn't get any help."

Nicholas opened his mouth to speak but was cut off by Becky. "Nic, we should talk about this as a group."

Nic turned to Becky, who was still seated inside the Suburban. Out of the corner of his eye, he saw Bryn roll her eyes.

Nicholas again was about to respond, this time to Becky, but again she interrupted, "We have to help if we can. Call the group together."

Nicholas grimaced and hollered, "Get the group together, quick meeting." He turned and saw everyone had already come together to see what was happening. He turned back and barked, "Colin, keep an eye on the boy."

Colin nodded.

When Abigail exited the Suburban, she turned to the boy and asked, "What's your name?"

He smiled and said, "Luke. My name is Luke."

While Colin kept a close eye on Luke, Nicholas pulled everyone together. He wanted to rush the meeting, as each second they sat still on the road left them vulnerable.

Before they had left San Diego, the group had agreed to give Nicholas the role of leader but had come to an understanding that the group would make decisions jointly if possible, specifically if it meant life or death, but wasn't an emergency.

Nicholas quickly explained the situation and called for a show of hands.

Those in favor of helping Luke were Abigail, Becky, Sophie, Proctor and his wife, Katherine; those opposed were Nicholas, Colin, Bryn, Abigail's boyfriend Rob, and Frank, with Marjorie standing by Frank, silent.

"Looks like we move on. I'm sorry, but like Bryn mentioned, we're a day out from safety. We can't sit here any longer than we have to," Nicholas said.

"Wait a second, Mom hasn't voted," Becky said,

challenging Nicholas.

"Of course she did, she voted with us," Frank snapped as he took Marjorie's arm.

Marjorie looked at Becky and held her head low.

"Mom, I can't believe you'd be in agreement on leaving this boy behind," Becky lamented.

Frank took a step towards the old Dodge Dart, but Marjorie refused to move.

"C'mon, Marj, time to load up, we're leaving."

"No!" she spat.

Her sharp reply to Frank made everyone's head turn.

"Frank, I love you, and I've agreed with you so many times in my life, but this time I can't. What kind of people are we if we just leave children alone and in need."

Frank went to respond, but not before Bryn fired back, "I'm sorry, but you don't know this kid, nor do I. We can't risk it. He could be walking us into an ambush or trap."

"He very well may be, but we need to take that risk, because if he's telling us the truth and we leave him and his poor sister to suffer, it doesn't make us any better than the bad guys that are roaming out there."

"Are you listening to yourself?" Bryn snapped.

Marjorie recoiled from Bryn's harsh response. She folded her arms and declared, "My vote is to help the boy."

Nicholas watched the back and forth right after Marjorie cast her vote. The entire thing made him feel sick to his stomach. He agreed with Bryn, he knew something was off about this and didn't want to take the risk, but he had also sworn to make their process as democratic as possible.

Unable to stop herself, Bryn skewered Marjorie and the others who voted to help. "Not one of you will be in the group to go look for this supposed girl. You have the easy vote, cast a vote, but someone else does the heavy lifting! Typical bullshit!"

"Not true, I'll go," Abigail said.

"Me too," Sophie followed.

Soon both groups began to talk over each other.

"Be quiet, everyone needs to be quiet!" Nicholas exclaimed.

All eyes turned to Nicholas and silence fell over the group.

"We agreed to vote on circumstances like this, and even though I think this idea is risky, I'll go along with it. Here's what's going to happen."

"Dad, I'll go," Abigail chimed in.

"No, that is not going to happen. I'll go and take Proctor with me."

"I don't think Proctor should go, he's needed. What if something happens to him?" Katherine objected.

"Sorry, but he goes. If this kid is right, we need his skills to bandage up the girl."

"I agree, send Colin," Becky said.

"No, and this decision is not a group vote. Proctor comes with me."

Proctor nervously looked around, hoping someone else would disagree, but everyone kept quiet. "Hey, Nic, I know I voted for us to go, and I'm not disagreeing, but it might be best if I stay."

"No, you're needed. The girl is hurt and she needs a

doctor. The last time I checked, that was you. Sorry, old buddy, but when you vote to do something you have to also reap the consequences," Nicholas said and walked towards Luke.

Bryn strode over to Proctor and Katherine and with a toothy grin said, "Next time you'll think twice before voting to risk people's lives."

Proctor exhaled deeply and headed towards the trailer to get his gear.

Nicholas watched the back and forth with Bryn and Proctor. He was tempted to chime in but decided the group didn't need his petty remarks; this wasn't to say he was pleased with his old friend's vote. He strode up to Colin and said, "If we don't come back in twelve hours, head north, go to the ranch, we'll catch up later."

"You sure?" Colin asked.

"Yeah, don't sit around waiting for us. I don't want any rescue missions. I can't risk my family, you take care of them."

"I don't think they'll agree to leave you behind, and Bryn, she'll be hard to stop too," Colin protested.

"Tell me you'll do as I wish."

Colin looked down; he was torn to give Nicholas his word but also understood the practicality of it.

"Promise me," Nicholas pressed.

"I'll take care of your family and get them to safety. I promise on my honor no harm will come to them," Colin solemnly declared.

"Also, if you hear anything that remotely sounds like a gun battle, leave. If anything at all makes you feel like the group is threatened, leave."

"Nic, I think you need to override this vote."

"I can't, this is what we decided back in Carlsbad, and I owe it to them to stick to the concept. Plus, this kid could be telling the truth."

"He's not a babe in the woods. He's gotta be fifteen or sixteen," Colin joked.

"We voted, we go. It's that simple because there could be someone in need; then we need to help them."

"But you know this is too risky."

"Yes, but it also might be slightly true."

"Listen, boss, even if it were true, you could still be walking into a hornet's nest. I encourage you to veto this."

"If we're going to build a future community, then I need to fulfill the group's wishes."

Colin shook his head.

"So we're good, you'll do as I say?"

"Yeah, but what happens if they call for a vote?"

"Ha, I'll leave that for you to figure out. Good man, thank you," Nicholas said and patted Colin on the shoulder.

Luke loudly cleared his throat.

Nicholas looked over at the young man and marched over to him.

Fear gripped Luke as Nicholas came within inches of his face.

"Looks like you got what you wanted."

"I can't thank you enough."

Nicholas grabbed him firmly by the arm and pulled him close. "Let me be very clear. If this is a trap, you'll be the first person I shoot, just remember that."

A cool breeze blew in and tussled Luke's thick sandy blond hair. With a shaky hand, he pushed the long bangs that covered his light blue eyes and said, "It's the truth, sir, I swear it."

Nicholas clenched his teeth and spat, "It better be the truth."

Undisclosed Bunker Facility, Superstition Mountains, East of Apache Junction, Arizona

For the third time in as many weeks, Michael found himself waking in a strange place, with injuries. The first time was on a beach, the second in a tiny children's bedroom, but this time was different, he found himself in what looked like a hospital room.

His vision was blurry and the dim overhead fluorescent lights didn't help. At the foot of his bed he made out the silhouette of someone.

"Where am I?" he asked.

The person stopped writing on the clipboard and immediately exited the room. The bright light from beyond his room splashed across the eggshell-white walls and laminate floors.

He tried to adjust his position in the bed but was stopped when he discovered his arms were secured by straps to the metal side railings. Several forceful attempts proved futile and he gave up.

The door again swung open, bringing in the light. He

looked and saw two people enter. They approached the foot of his bed and stood.

"How are you feeling?" a woman said.

Michael squinted to make out who it was but was unable to, but the voice he recognized. It was the woman from the crash and from his dreams. "Karina?"

"Yes, sweetheart, it's me," she replied.

Next to her, a tall man leaned in and whispered to Karina.

"No, let him rest more," Karina replied back to the man.

Michael couldn't make out what the man said, but he feared it wasn't good.

More of his memory had returned, but it still wasn't complete. He remembered being with her and that they had been romantic but nothing more, and based upon his situation, there was definitely more. Ever since he'd washed up on the shores of the Sea of Cortez, he had wanted to know why, and for the first time he was with someone who knew him and could help fill in the empty spaces of his life.

"Where am I?" he asked her.

She approached the side of the bed and took his hand in hers.

Her warm touch coupled with her presence made him feel secure. Seeing her tall, lean body brought back memories of them together, wrapped in each other's embrace.

"Just rest, sweetheart, you've been through a lot."

"I can't remember a lot. Why am I here?"

"It's a long story."

"Why did you crash into my car?"

"We didn't; that was some of Viktor's men," she answered.

"I don't understand."

"We were following them. We knew they were tracking you. Had we known they were going to ram you, we would have stopped them sooner."

"I don't understand," he said again. "Why is someone trying to kill me?"

The man blurted out something in Russian and from his tone he sounded upset.

Karina turned and replied in Russian.

Michael was confused; he looked to Karina and asked, "What did he say?"

"Not for you to worry about, what is important is that you rest. Soon we'll talk, but for now, rest."

"Okay, but can you remove the restraints?" Michael asked.

The man again said something in Russian.

Karina snapped at the man in Russian, then turned to Michael and said, "Of course, but do you promise you'll be good."

"Of course. I don't even know where I am. How can I do any harm?"

"You're restrained because you hurt a few nurses," the man charged.

"I did?"

"Unfortunately, yes, you did."

"Are they okay?" Michael asked, concerned that he might have unintentionally hurt an innocent person.

"Karina, this is not a good idea. We can't be sure he won't hurt someone again."

"I don't remember, I swear, there must have been a reason," Michael said, defending his actions.

"It was the drugs he was on and the traumatic events he lived through recently," Karina replied, she too defending Michael's actions while under the influence of hardcore narcotics.

"Why did you give me drugs?" Michael asked.

"Yes, you were a bit upset and not yourself when we brought you here," Karina said. Her tone softened when she talked to Michael.

"I promise I won't do anything. I'll cooperate fully," Michael said. He meant what he said only halfheartedly; he just wanted the restraints off.

The man stood like a statue, obviously contemplating the request. "Fine, but he's your responsibility, do you understand?"

Karina unbuckled the thick leather restraints and took a step back for caution's sake once he was free.

Michael rubbed his wrists, happy to be free to move around.

The man gave Michael a hard look and moved his right hand to a pistol holstered on his hip, giving Michael a clear clue as to what he would do if he tried anything.

"Where am I?" Michael asked Karina.

"Get some rest and we'll talk more tomorrow."

Michael was desperate to know more. "And who is that?"

"That's Anatoly; he looks and acts like he's angry all

the time, but trust me, he's a teddy bear."

Anatoly glared at her.

Karina stepped forward again and bent down. Her long black hair fell onto Michael's face as she gave him a kiss on the cheek. "Get some rest."

"I will and thank you," Michael replied, holding up his freed hands.

Anatoly and Karina walked to the door. Just before she stepped out, Karina turned back and said, "Welcome back, I missed you."

Vista, CA

Vincent hadn't seen another person since watching Roger and his family leave. At first he dealt with the solitude, fully expecting to encounter some straggler or wandering person coming up to the compound, looking for a handout, but no one came. He could only imagine the neighbors were too frightened to return. Not having one person show up seemed odd, but not so much that it troubled him. Not having to deal with anyone was nice.

It had taken him only half a day to pack one of the SUVs for his eventual departure, so his remaining days had been spent hobbling around the property on patrol. Using the satellite phone Roger left him, he tried calling his parents, but all he got was a pulsing tone indicating the system was down. Many times he thought about his unit and wondered what they were doing. Not a day would go by without him contemplating returning to Camp Pendleton, but his intimate knowledge of Marine life and the Marine Corps in general allowed him to squash those thoughts. He had one chance to go help his parents, and if he ended back up at Camp Pendleton, they'd put him to task right after he healed. This was his only opportunity and he would take it.

A small grove of mature avocado trees sat near the north end of the property on a sloping hill. The climb to the top was difficult for him, but once he crested the hill, it proved worthwhile. His spot atop the hill gave him a great vantage point of the property, house and outbuildings below as well as a view of the surrounding area, plus he enjoyed the cool westerly breeze that blew off the ocean beyond.

He leaned against a large rock and stretched out his right leg so he'd have blood flow easily to it. Looking at his heavily bandaged foot, he cracked a smile at his dumb luck. In his entire career as a Marine he hadn't heard of very many people surviving a helicopter crash, but he had. He didn't know the odds, but he figured if he had been successful with the odds while playing the lottery he'd be a millionaire, but what good would the money be now. He had been so fortunate that when his luck came, it had saved his life and put him in a position to go help his family. He loved the Marine Corps and his daily doubts about his not returning would come in waves, but what good was he or what kind of son was he if he couldn't defend his family? He had joined the Marines for a variety of reasons, one of those being to protect his loved ones from the evil that existed in the world. But now that evil had descended on his country and his parents were threatened. He didn't know how long he'd be dogged with these doubts, but the emotional tug of Idaho and his family won out every time.

It seemed so strange to look out on the rolling hills and see the modern world, but the sounds of that world were gone, almost as if someone had hit the mute button. His world was now filled with the sounds of chirping birds and rustling leaves. Occasionally he'd hear the familiar crack of gunfire, but it was always too far away to give him much concern.

He enjoyed the combination of the warm sun and cool breeze. There were many things he disliked about Southern California; one thing he loved was the weather. How could you beat it? he'd often mentioned before. He never understood those friends from eastern or Midwestern states who had both bad weather and bad politics. He often joked to those friends that if you were going to live in a place where your personal liberties were lessened, at least make it nice outside.

The one problem he found with his perch was the combination of warm sun and cool breeze would stoke his desire to nap. Again, he was fighting the feeling when a movement near the gate caught his attention. He opened his eyes wide but didn't move anything else. Like a laser beam, he focused on the spot for minutes, but nothing moved. He began to wonder if he had imagined it. As more minutes passed, he came to the conclusion it had been a near-sleep dream.

"I swear I saw something," he whispered under his

breath as he placed his binoculars to his eyes. He scanned the area but saw nothing, He focused intently on the gate but saw no one or anything out of the norm. More minutes passed and just as he was about to give up, he saw the movement again. This time there was no doubt as he watched a young child scale the gate and jump into the compound, followed by a woman.

"I knew I wasn't seeing shit," he muttered. Reflexively he went to get up but was quickly reminded about his handicap. "This damn foot is such a pain in my ass." Using a crutch and the rock, he lifted himself. Once steady, he began his slow descent. Every few feet, he'd stop and scan the compound, hoping to see their location and if anyone else had come over. Unfortunately, he hadn't seen them since they came in and hadn't seen anyone else.

With his current physical condition, it took him ten times as long to get down the hill and near the back door of the house. Sweat poured off his brow and streamed down his face. His T-shirt was soaked and his breathing was labored. At the back door he paused and listened for any signs they were close. Not hearing them, he turned the doorknob and slowly pushed it open. With as much speed as he could muster, he hopped inside, turned and ran directly into the young woman.

She screamed and pushed him hard.

Not able to get good footing, he tumbled and fell backwards. He hit the floor with a thud, the back of his head smacking against the hard wood.

The woman didn't advance. With terror in her voice, she cried out, "Noah, get out of the house, hurry!"

Vincent could see the fear on her face but didn't see her as a threat until she pulled out the pistol.

"You just lie right there; don't think about attacking me. I'll shoot you, I swear to you, don't test me!"

Even if Vincent wanted to resist or stop her, he couldn't. His splayed position on the floor prevented him from countering her. If she wanted to, she could kill him right there; however, he sensed she wasn't a killer. "Please don't shoot me. I'm not going to hurt you," Vincent said, raising his hands, palms out towards her.

Her hands were shaking and sweat dripped off her glistening face. "We only came looking for medicine, that's all. Now, you stay there so we can leave, okay?"

"Fine, that's fine, but maybe I can help. Who needs medicine?"

Around the corner, a young boy, not seven years old, came sprinting.

"Noah, I told you to go!" the woman screamed.

"I, uh, I didn't understand you. I thought you needed help!" Noah cried as he stopped in his tracks upon seeing Vincent.

"I won't hurt you, and if you need help, you came to the right place," Vincent called out, his hands still up.

"Do you have any antibiotics?" the woman asked, the muzzle of her pistol still aimed at Vincent.

"Yes."

"Where?"

"I'll take you there."

"No, tell me where!" she screamed.

"It's located in a cabinet and it's locked."

"Where are the keys?"

"I won't hurt you and I know first aid."

"Where are the keys?" she asked and took a step closer. "I'll shoot you, I swear!"

"What good would that do you?"

"Why shouldn't I?"

"Why should you?"

"You can't trust anyone these days, especially men."

All Vincent could imagine was she had been hurt, maybe even raped. There could be no other reason for her skepticism.

He lowered his hand to dig in his pocket for the keys.

She pulled the trigger. A chunk of wall and sheet rock flew through the air. The loud shot hurt his ears and, from her expression, hers too.

Noah rapidly put his hands to his ears and moaned.

"Easy!" Vincent yelled.

"Put your hands back up, or I'll shoot you next time!" she ordered.

"I was going into my pocket to get you the keys," Vincent explained.

She furrowed her brow. "Go ahead, get the keys," she said and motioned with the pistol.

Slowly he lowered his hand, dug into his pocket and pulled out a ring of keys. He tossed them over to her and said, "Look in the garage, third cabinet on the right. There's a fridge in there. Take what you need."

He then remembered he had emptied the refrigerator of most of the medicine save for fifteen bottles of prenatal vitamins, two bottles of melatonin and twenty packets of birth control. Items he didn't imagine he'd need.

She squatted down, never taking the pistol off him, and picked up the keys. She looked at them, then him and asked, "How do I know you won't follow me in there and do something?"

"I won't and don't even think about tying me up. I've given you the damn keys and my word. Go get what you want and get the hell out of here," Vincent responded.

"Noah, here, go to the garage and find that fridge. Put every bottle of medicine you find in a bag. Call for me when you're done."

Noah approached and snatched the keys. He looked at the woman then turned his eyes to Vincent.

Vincent nodded and gave him a wink.

Noah returned Vincent's nod with a slight one of his own, then turned and ran away just as fast as he had appeared.

"Thank you," Vincent said as he rested his head on the floor.

"For what?" she asked.

"For not tying me up."

"Who says I won't do that?"

He looked up and saw a slight grin on her face.

"I don't know what happened to you, but I'm not that guy. I'm actually one of the good ones."

"No such thing."

"Well whatever happened, I'm sorry it happened. The world has turned to shit, and soon you'll come to realize that we good people have to stick together, because the lone wolf won't survive."

"Whatever." She smirked.

"What's your name?" he asked.

"Nunea."

"Nunea?"

"Yeah, nunea damn business."

He chuckled and once again rested his head back on the cool floor.

Minutes went by like hours.

"I got everything, Mom," Noah hollered from further in the house.

"Looks like we have to say goodbye," the woman said as she tucked the pistol in her waistband.

"Nice meeting you too," Vincent said mockingly.

She turned around, and just before making the corner, she gave him one last look then disappeared.

By her heavy footfalls he could tell she was running away. He sat up and exhaled deeply. "I haven't seen anyone in days, and when I do, they hold me up. You're losing it, Vincent, you're really losing it."

Four miles southwest of Wellsville, Utah

"Can we take a short break?" Luke asked, bent over in exhaustion.

Nicholas, who was following Luke's lead, stopped and said, "No, we keep moving."

"My left foot hurts bad and my knee feels like it's grinding against bone. Please, just a short break?" Luke pleaded.

Nicholas looked around. They were standing in an open area surrounded by a thick grove of tall shrubs and trees. Their visibility was ten to twelve feet at most.

"Give the boy a break. I could use one too," Proctor added.

Nicholas leered at Proctor and kept surveying their surroundings. He didn't like stopping where they were. In fact, he wished now he had put his foot down and refused to go on this fool's mission. "I don't want to stop. Let's keep pressing forward."

"One second," Luke said as he began to put his left shoe back on.

"Hurry up," Nicholas ordered; he pulled a gold pocket watch from his pants and with his thumb pressed the latch release. The shiny yellow gold popped open to reveal the white-faced watch and bold black hands. He glanced at the time and put the watch away quickly.

"Argh," Luke grunted as he slid his shoe back on.

"Is your foot bleeding?" Proctor asked and approached Luke, who had ignored Nicholas and had sat down and removed his shoe.

"Yeah, some blisters burst," Luke answered.

"For fuck's sake, just suck it up. How far away do you think we are?"

Sweat streamed off Luke's face. He again ignored Nicholas and took off his shoe for Proctor to examine his blisters.

"How far?" Nicholas pressed.

"A mile or so."

"Or so?"

"Yeah."

Proctor stripped off his pack and pulled out a first aid kit.

"That was cool. I haven't seen anyone use an old-fashioned watch like that," Luke commented.

Nicholas didn't pay attention to Luke's small talk.

Proctor pulled off Luke's bloody sock and tossed it aside.

"Is he always grumpy?" Luke asked Proctor.

"He's focused not grumpy," Proctor replied.

"Hmm, seems grumpy to me. I was only asking him about his watch. It's really cool."

"He got it from his brother not two weeks before everything went to hell," Proctor said.

"Let's not discuss my private life," Nicholas blurted out.

To the left of them, a branch cracked. Everyone grew silent and Nicholas leaned in and began to intently scan the area.

Proctor stopped giving aid and also looked in the direction the sound had come from.

The sound of leaves crunching then came from their right.

Nicholas put his rifle to his shoulder and pivoted around in that direction.

The expression on Proctor's face turned to concern when he saw Nicholas spin around. He went to get up but was stopped when he felt cold metal pushed up under his chin. He froze and lowered his eyes to see the pistol in

Luke's hand.

"Don't move," Luke ordered.

Nicholas heard the commotion and turned. "I fucking knew it!" he blurted out and faced Luke and Proctor, rifle out in front of him. "Drop the gun."

Loud crashing came from all directions.

"You're surrounded; you'll die if you try anything!" Luke exclaimed.

Nicholas could feel his blood boil and his instincts told him to begin firing. He then saw several men emerge from the shrub line. They were camouflaged and heavily armed. He placed his sights on each as they came forth, and the desire to start killing them was present, but he remained disciplined. He knew he couldn't win this fight as he saw more and more break through and advance on him. By a rough count he was outnumbered by over dozen.

"Drop your rifle," Luke ordered.

"I knew you were lying, I knew it," Nicholas spat.

"I didn't want to do this, I promise. They forced me. They said they'd kill my sister," Luke responded in a weak attempt to have Nicholas understand his dilemma.

"I should fucking kill you right now," Nicholas barked.

"You won't be killing anyone, you understand," a rough voice said behind Nicholas.

Nicholas felt the muzzle of a rifle pressed against the back of his head.

"Drop the rifle, now," the man ordered.

"I'll drop it," Nicholas said calmly as he pointed his rifle to the sky and pulled the trigger, firing a single shot, hoping to signal the group that they were in trouble.

"Idiot!" the man barked.

Nicholas dropped the rifle, closed his eyes and waited for what was coming next.

The man quickly struck Nicholas with the butt of his rifle.

Nicholas grunted in pain and fell to the ground.

U.S. Highway 91, six miles southwest of Wellsville, Utah

The distant single crack of gunfire echoed off the hills surrounding them, giving everyone pause.

Becky looked up, her eyes wide in anticipation of hearing more shots, but none came.

Colin's body tensed. He raised his rifle and readied for someone to burst from the tree line.

Bryn jumped up and, like Colin, prepared to do battle, her pistol drawn.

"Do you think that was them?" Becky asked.

"Hard to tell, but we have to assume it was," Colin replied, his eyes still on the trees below.

"I agree with Colin. We have to assume it was," Bryn commented.

"What do we do?" Becky asked.

"We wait," Katherine declared.

Colin looked at his watch and said, "We wait for now, but we need to remain vigilant."

"Is that possible?" Bryn joked. "We're sitting here on a road just begging to be shot, robbed and raped and not necessarily in that order."

"Why does she always have to be crude," Marjorie blurted out.

"Crude? What's crude is your ass-backwards thinking. Is it more humane to risk our lives for strangers we don't know?"

"Yes, it is humane. I don't want to live in a world where the people I know lose their humanity."

"Humanity, humane, all these noble words, but I don't see you out there risking your life to save what could be a fake person. It's one thing to save someone we know or know if it's real. This entire thing could be a trap and your vote could have put them all in the sights of predators and cutthroats," Bryn snapped.

"Really, I am just astonished at your language and disgusting behavior!" Marjorie blared.

Bryn raised her left hand and folded her fingers into a fist. With her right hand she acted like she was reeling in line on a fishing rod. Each turn of her right hand brought the index finger of her left higher and higher. When her finger was raised, she blew Marjorie a kiss.

"You're repulsive!" Marjorie moaned, then walked into the trailer and slammed the door.

Frank looked at Bryn but didn't say a word. His expressionless face gave no clue as to what he thought about Bryn and Marjorie's clash.

Becky, however, couldn't let their bickering go without adding her thoughts. "Bryn, please leave her alone."

"I know she's your mother, but I'm not sorry. This bleeding-heart bullshit might kill us."

"You can disagree, but you don't have to be so…"

Bryn raised her eyebrows and cocked her head.

"Becky, if you think you're going to convince my sister to change her mind or tactics, forget it. She's been hardheaded since she was born," Sophie chimed in.

"I love you too," Bryn responded to Sophie.

"People, stop the bickering. It doesn't help!" Colin chided.

"Colin's right. We need to keep our minds free of these little battles and focused," Katherine said. She walked over to Becky and offered her hand.

Becky took it.

Katherine caressed it and said, "We'll wait. Our husbands are fine. They're tough men and smart; they'll be back soon." Katherine and Becky had met many years ago at a charity event and since then had been friends. If it hadn't been for their friendship, Proctor and Nicholas wouldn't have met. Their personalities clashed sometimes, but deep down they shared common values and outlooks on life.

Becky remained sitting and looked up at Katherine's golden hair, which she now wore pulled back into a ponytail. Becky had joked recently that the ponytail and makeup-less faces of women was the new *look* for the coming years.

Abigail walked up to Becky and Katherine. She couldn't hide the fear and worry, it was written all over her face. Her youthful and smooth skin was creased with anxious concern and she found herself doubting her decision.

Rob had attempted to console her, but it hadn't worked. Since their departure, Rob had begun to feel like he wasn't needed, and this was yet another time where he tried to be of value and she turned away from him. He began to wonder if their relationship or what they had before was gone with the world before.

"Come here, baby," Becky said, motioning for Abigail to take a seat next to her.

"Mom, I think we messed up," Abigail said, referring to the vote to go help Luke.

"Let's not start second-guessing. Like Katherine said, they're strong and smart men," Becky said, trying to make Abigail feel better, but she wondered if it was herself she was trying to convince.

"I'm just scared for Daddy, and hearing the gunshot made me worry more. I heard what Bryn said, and maybe she's right. Here we are trying to do what we think is right, but that was for a different time."

"That's nonsense," Katherine interjected.

"But what if it is? What I mean is our morals came from a time when there weren't the types of risks we have today. Maybe we need to adjust?"

"I'm with Marjorie. We can't leave our humanity behind," Katherine said.

"But is it humane to get our family killed trying to save someone we don't know? How do we really know if there is someone that needs to be saved?" Abigail asked.

Katherine paused; she was about to counter Abigail when she decided to just let what she said sink in.

"Life was easy before, we could sit in the luxury or

safety of our lives and make easy claims of belief in humanity, but we never had to actually do anything, we never had to risk anything. Now we do and the cost might be too much."

Katherine opened her mouth to speak but again cut herself off. She thought for a moment then said, "You make some valid points."

Becky heard what she was saying, and it wasn't any different than what Bryn had said or what Nicholas had said, but the way Abigail was saying it made it sink in.

Bryn listened to the women talking and wanted to tell them that it was too late for second-guessing. She walked over to Colin and said, "What's the plan if we don't hear from them?"

"If they don't come back in ten hours, we pop smoke and head north."

"Pop smoke?"

"Leave, we leave."

"We're not leaving anyone; we go find them. That's what we do."

Colin looked at her and asked, "What has gotten into you? You've become quite the bitter and angry hard-ass. Where's that tough but still composed girl I use to know?"

"I'm still that girl."

"I'm not so sure, you're getting into arguments with old ladies, you're cursing and now yelling at people in our group."

"I just can't sit around and listen to stupid. I listened to it before the shit hit the fan, but now stupid and antiquated ideas can get us killed."

"I can't disagree with you on that, but how about toning down some of your rhetoric. We do have to live with these people. And if I remember, didn't Nicholas save you and your sister?"

"Yeah, but that was different."

"How?"

"It was different; he was there witnessing it. We don't know for sure if there is a girl; that's a huge difference."

"But he still risked his life to save you."

She wanted to counter what he said, but let it process in her mind. She respected his opinion and had him to thank for so much. In her life she had many rocky relationships with men and had all but given up on believing that men could be trusted, but found three men recently that had shattered that belief. First, there was Matt, the one guy she never expected to show strength and courage. Then Colin presented himself and gave her instruction and the tools needed to survive, and finally there was Nicholas, who saved her just when she needed it. She owed all her life to those men and swore she'd repay that debt later.

"I hate to admit it, but you might be right. I'm just stressed. I don't like the traveling; I just want to get where we're going. I just feel like every turn or small shit town will spell disaster for us; then this happens with that kid. It's not like I'm heartless, I just don't feel it. I think that kid's lying and we just democratically voted to send off two of our own to go get killed."

"Don't underestimate Nic. he's a tough son of a bitch and Proctor seems able. However, that's not to say their invincible."

"So what do you make of that gunshot?"

"Could be them, could be coincidence. It's a violent world out there."

"So you're giving them ten more hours then we leave?" Bryn asked.

"Not my choice, that was Nic's orders and I promised to do what he instructed."

"I don't think I can leave them, I just don't think I can do that," Bryn said, looking off into the thick forest beyond.

Colin looked at his watch and said, "If they're not back in nine hours and forty-eight minutes, we're pushing north to the ranch. Once everyone is safe, we can discuss sending a team back, but let's just hope it doesn't come to that."

"Yeah, let's hope. You hungry?"

"A bite of food sounds good right now."

"I'll be right back," Bryn said and strutted off.

Colin again looked at his watch. It was agony watching the seconds bleed into minutes. The single gunshot told him that something bad happened to them. He obviously didn't know for sure, he just felt it in his gut.

A ray of light found a break in the heavy cloud cover and shined down at his feet. He looked up and watched the clouds move quickly to cover up the small hole. Under his breath he muttered, "You better come back, Nic, you better come back."

Four miles southwest of Wellsville, Utah

A deep and painful throbbing emanated from Nicholas' head and spanned from the back to the front. He was drifting in and out of consciousness. Strange voices and laughter filled his ears, making for nightmares while he was out, until a loud crash jolted him fully awake. He opened his stinging eyes to find he was on the ground and tied up. He looked around to see where Proctor might be, but he couldn't find him. Not far off he saw a small campfire, and around it was the men who had attacked them.

Nicholas' struggling had caught the attention of one of his captors. He walked away from the campfire and stood over him. "Look who's awake." The man bent down and grabbed him forcibly by the arm, pulled him up and placed him on his butt.

Nicholas was impressed with the man's strength.

"Hey, guys, that dude is awake," the man informed his friends.

More of the men left the fire to reacquaint themselves with Nicholas.

Nicholas would be lying to himself if he didn't admit he was afraid of what was going to happen to him. He prayed that torture wasn't their modus operandi.

"You suppose he's ready to help us?" one of the men asked.

"He better be if he knows what's good for him," the leader of the group said as he pushed his way past his men and stopped just in front of Nicholas.

"Are you willing to cooperate with us?" the man asked Nicholas.

Throughout his life, Nicholas found it just about impossible to focus when he had a major headache, and this was one of those times.

One of the men kicked him and asked, "You awake?"

Nicholas grunted.

"Ha, Cam really hit him hard; the motherfucker can only mumble shit." The man laughed.

Nicholas heard and understood the man clearly and it irritated him. "Fuck you," he whispered under his breath.

"Huh? What did you say?" the man asked, bending over to listen.

Nicholas raised his head to meet the man's eyes and repeated, "Fuck you!"

"Fuck me? Um, I don't think that's going to happen, but you, on the other hand, you're pretty much fucked unless you help us."

Nicholas remained defiant and angry. He snorted and spit out a large wad of phlegm. "You're a dead man."

"This guy is a jokester." The man laughed then kicked Nicholas in the side.

Nicholas cringed from the pain and fell onto his side.

The man again kicked him.

"Leave him be. We need him as healthy as possible," the man known as Cam hollered. He approached his men and pushed them away. "Go back to the fire and settle down. You two stay here."

His men did as he instructed, with the one man walking away laughing.

Cam reached down and picked Nicholas up. "You all right?"

All Nicholas could do was nod. He thought about being resistant, but with his arms bound, he'd accomplish nothing but further abuse. He now thought it best to see what they wanted and to find out if he could get out of his predicament.

"Good, are you able to understand me and talk?" Cam asked.

Again Nicholas nodded.

"You're probably wondering why we've kidnapped you. Well, it's very simple. We need vehicles and you have them."

Nicholas' head throbbed terribly and was so painful he was having a difficult time focusing. When he opened his eyes, the simple light of day hurt.

"So you see, we need you to go and convince your friends to give up. We don't want to fight for them; we want you to hand them over. We don't want bloodshed; we just want your vehicles. You see, it's very simple, just give them to us. I know that getting into a skirmish we run the chance of damaging the vehicles, so it's a better idea if we can get them fully operational."

Mustering his strength, Nicholas replied, "I can't do that."

"I had a feeling you'd say that," Cam said and stood. He walked behind Nicholas and grabbed Proctor, who was also restrained and gagged.

Proctor struggled, but Cam forcibly brought him in front of Nicholas. With a kick to the back of the knee,

Proctor fell down.

Both Proctor and Nicholas looked at each other.

Nicholas could see fear in Proctor's eyes. He wondered if he had that same look.

"I know you're the leader, so it only makes sense that I torture your friend here until you accept my terms," Cam said as he pulled out a long sheath knife and placed it on Proctor's cheek.

The cold steel of the blade made Proctor quiver.

"You have one last chance to say you're going to help, or I begin to carve your friend up," Cam said, his tone now turning sinister.

Proctor mumbled from behind the gag, and his eyes told Nicholas that he didn't want to get hurt. However, giving in to these men's wishes could lead to his group dying. Vehicles were critical and he couldn't trust these men. How did he know they'd honor any deal? He didn't, and by the look of the daylight, he estimated they'd been gone for several hours now. Nicholas had only one option, stall for time and, while he did that, find a way to escape.

"I'm going to count to three," Cam said as he caressed Proctor's cheek with the blade. "One, two…"

Proctor's eyes began to widen with each count. His chest heaved in anticipation of the cold steel cutting through his warm face.

"Don't," Nicholas said.

"What was that?" Cam asked.

"Don't hurt him. I'll help you."

Proctor exhaled deeply, relieved that he wouldn't have to suffer from the torture Cam had in store for him.

"Good choice. You see, I really don't want hurt anyone. I just want your vehicles so my men and I can head west," Cam said. He began to pull away from Proctor but allowed the blade to nip his cheek.

Proctor recoiled from the superficial cut.

"Oops, sorry," Cam said with a devilish grin.

Several of his men laughed then walked back to the small campfire.

Nicholas shot Cam a hard look then turned his attention to Proctor, who looked as happy as one could be considering their situation.

"Can you remove his gag?" Nicholas asked.

"Sure," Cam responded and ordered one of his men to take it off.

With the gag removed, Proctor spit and moved his jaw around. A small trickle of blood streamed down his right cheek.

"You all right?" Nicholas asked.

"Yeah," Proctor answered.

Nicholas looked at Cam and began to really size him up. He was a large man, well over six feet, with wide shoulders and thick arms. His clothes were soiled and what skin was exposed was streaked with dirt and grime. He and his men had the appearance that they'd been living off the land for a while.

"Any way we can get something to eat?" Nicholas asked.

"I don't see why not," Cam said and motioned to one of his men to get something.

"Where's the kid who led us here?" Nicholas asked,

looking around.

"The little shit took off with his sister. He's a sly one, just like his old man," Cam said.

Nicholas thought this odd. "He wasn't with your group?"

"Hell no, that little snot was from that shit hole a few miles north. We snatched them hoping we could use them in exchange if the townspeople caught up with us, but he came in handy as bait instead."

Nicholas got this sense that the men were on the run. "Are those townspeople coming after you?"

Cam squatted down and said, "I'll say this because I'm a nice guy, so I'll give you a sound bit of advice. Those people are more depraved than this pack of assholes." Cam then pointed to his men around the fire.

One of Cam's men walked up and tossed wrapped granola bars on the ground in front of Nicholas. "Bon appétit."

"Are you going to feed us?" Nicholas asked rhetorically as he turned to show his bound wrists.

"Untie them," Cam ordered. "But don't even think about anything stupid," he then said to Proctor and Nicholas.

"I wouldn't think of it."

With their arms unbound, Nicholas and Proctor tore open the wrappers and began to devour the bars.

"When you're done with those, we'll go get my vehicles," Cam said and walked off but left one of his men to stand guard over them.

With his mouth full, Proctor asked, "You sure this is a

good idea?"

"Would you rather I let him carve you up?"

"Ah, no."

"How about a bit of thanks."

"You're right, thank you."

"It's going to be a long walk north."

"Can we get some water? These things are like sawdust," Nicholas asked.

"Argh, you guys are a pain in the ass. Don't you run," he grunted and walked away to get water.

"What, are we going to hop away?" Nicholas snorted, referring to their ankles still being bound.

With him gone, Nicholas leaned in and quietly said, "I have no intention of giving them our vehicles, just buying time here."

"So what's your plan?"

Nicholas stuffed half a bar into his mouth and answered honestly, "I don't have one, yet."

Cam had given Proctor and Nicholas an hour to rest before coming forward to tell them what was next.

"Now that you've had time to plan whatever bullshit you think you'll try, let me dash those plans," Cam said and pulled a handheld radio from his belt. Before he pressed the button, he said, "We found a prepper who had these neatly tucked away in some box. I'm so grateful for people like him; he was ready for this sort of thing."

Nicholas knew Cam's type; they were the marauders he had heard would roam after an event like the one they were living. They never had any intention of preparing; they would arm themselves and then set upon others and steal.

Cam broadly smiled, showing his yellow-stained teeth and reddish gums. He keyed the radio and said, "Ben, this is Cam. Tell me, what do you see?"

Nicholas had a sick feeling, as he knew where Ben was.

"I see a big nigger and a few bitches running around. Nothing new since last time."

"How many vehicles and what type?" Cam asked.

"Some old sedan and a Suburban with a trailer."

Cam again grinned and said, "Is that enough incentive for you two not to try anything? Cause if you do, I won't have a choice but to open up on your little group."

A wave of clashing emotions came over Nicholas. At first he wanted to lunge for Cam and beat him senseless, but that was quickly tempered when he thought of Becky and Abigail in the crosshairs of Ben.

"I hear you, we won't try anything," Nicholas lamented.

"We hear you," Proctor added.

"Good, now get them up, boys, we have a little hike ahead of us," Cam ordered.

Nicholas could think more clearly now that his headache had subsided, but he strained to come up with a plan of escape. One obstacle he hadn't counted on was Cam having a man on site and within radio range. If he tried to attack them, it could lead to a simple call on the radio, which would definitely lead to deadly consequences for the group.

Right now his options had dwindled to just slowing them down, but how? They crested a steep hill and what lay ahead was a steep decline into a small valley. He remembered the terrain from their hike out there. They were not far now. Once past the valley, they were only a mile away from the group. He had to find a way to slow them down and the only way was to feign injury.

A large branch lay in front of him several steps down the hill, and if he tripped over it, he'd allow gravity to do the rest. With no other options, he took those steps, jammed an ankle under the branch and fell forward. He hit the ground hard, his chest and right shoulder taking the brunt of the fall. He whipped around and began to roll. All around him he heard the yells of Cam's men. As he spun down the hill, he began to feel a bit nauseous; then suddenly he stopped, his side slamming into a large tree. The pain was excruciating, but he hoped it would buy him time.

Cam ran down and yelled, "What the hell?"

Nicholas slowly got to his knees but doubled over in pain.

"You're a clumsy idiot. Now get up," Cam barked.

"Give me a sec, I hurt my ribs." Nicholas coughed.

Cam grunted his displeasure and hollered to several of his men, "Get over here and help him."

Proctor jogged over and knelt next to Nicholas. "That was some fall, you all right?"

Nicholas coughed and spit out some blood. "Um, I think I really hurt myself."

"Just what we need," Proctor quipped.

"Get him up," Cam ordered his men, who surrounded Nicholas and pulled him to his feet.

Once standing, Nicholas bent over in pain. "Argh, fuck, I really think I broke a rib."

"Does it hurt when you take a breath?" Proctor asked.

"Yes, and it just hurts."

"What, are you a doctor or something?" Cam asked.

"Actually, yes, I am."

"We don't have time for this. Let's get moving," Cam yelled.

"Let me examine him first," Proctor said.

Cam looked up at the sky then back to them. "You have five minutes and then we move."

"Sit back down," Proctor ordered Nicholas.

Nicholas did exactly what Proctor said, all the while grimacing in pain.

As Proctor was examining him, Nicholas smiled at the irony of the entire situation.

"What is so funny?" Proctor asked.

"I knew this entire mission was shit, but I just thought that I should be a good guy and allow our little democracy a chance. Wow, what a mistake that was."

"Well, if I could take it all back, I would. Next time, please smack me upside the head."

"If we get out of this alive, I plan on kicking your stupid ass," Nicholas joked.

"Enough grab ass! Get up, we're moving!" Cam yelled.

"I need another minute," Proctor replied.

"No, get up, we move!" Cam barked and took a step towards them but stopped suddenly when his head exploded.

Shocked by this unexpected attack but knowing what to do, Nicholas grabbed Proctor by his shirt and ordered, "Get down."

Cam's men reacted quickly; they faced the direction of the single gunshot and started firing.

Their volley was matched by whoever was ambushing them with the difference being those attacking were hitting their targets squarely. One by one, Cam's men were getting fatally hit and dropping. Those who remained returned fire, but it didn't stop the relentless hail of fire from those hidden.

Nicholas and Proctor curled up against the large tree and took cover as bullets ripped past them. Nicholas was tempted to run, but they were caught in a crossfire. If they were to stand, they would most surely be hit.

Bark and splinters of wood exploded off the tree they were using for cover as bullets from both sides hit it.

Nicholas felt a sharp pain in his lower right side, just below the ribs he had either bruised or broken. He then felt something warm and wet running down his side. He placed his hand there and pulled it back to see it was covered with blood. "Argh," he grunted in pain and frustration.

Suddenly, the gunfire stopped and silence returned to the forest.

Although he was in tremendous pain, he knew this was the opportunity to make a run for it. "This is our chance," Nicholas said and grabbed Proctor, but he didn't move. He looked over his shoulder and saw he was motionless. He rolled him over and saw a bloody hole in his chest. Ignoring his own pain, he knelt over his friend and ripped open his shirt only to discover an errant bullet had struck Proctor, and by its location, it looked like it went through the heart. "Ah, no," he cried out as he jammed two fingers on Proctor's throat to check his carotid artery for a pulse. He found nothing.

Nicholas blinked heavily to focus his sight, which had become blurry. His head began to spin, nausea twisted his stomach, and a cold sweat clung to his forehead. He tried to think, but his thoughts were muddled. Frustrated, in pain and losing blood, he tried to calm himself. Again he blinked heavily, but it did no good. Soon he'd be face down. Lost in a fog, he didn't hear the footsteps behind him.

"Is your friend hurt?" a voice asked.

Nicholas slowly turned around to find two men in ghillie suits. He opened his mouth but only mumbled something unintelligible. He went to get up, but the vertigo finally took over and he passed out.

U.S. Highway 91, six miles southwest of Wellsville, Utah

The gunshots reverberated off the hills and caused a panic with the group.

Becky bolted from the Suburban and ran over to Colin. "That has to be them."

"Hard to know, but we do have to assume it is," Colin replied, his eyes glued on the tree line.

Bryn took up a defensive position behind the old

Dodge.

Katherine, Abigail, Marjorie and Frank all huddled together just outside the trailer.

Rob followed Bryn's example and, with a bolt-action rifle, stood in front of the Suburban, covering the road ahead of them.

The gunfire stopped as suddenly as it had happened. The silence of the group and their surroundings was intense.

Becky whispered, "What should we do?"

"Sssh," Colin snapped. He leaned his head forward and listened.

Nervously she did as he asked and just stood next to him.

The crackle of a radio handset came from a grouping of large shrubs below them and caught his ear. He whispered to Becky, "Get behind me."

Becky did as he asked without question.

He raised his rifle to his face and looked through his optics in the direction of the sound.

The deafening crack of a rifle jolted Colin and Becky.

A towering figure stepped from within the trees and stopped several feet from the incline. He wavered and dropped to his knees.

Colin swung the rifle towards the man and settled his crosshairs on his chest to see blood pouring from a wound.

"Fucking die!" Bryn said as she squeezed off another round.

The bullet ripped through the man's chest. The force of the 5.56mm round caused his limp body to fall backwards.

Frank, Marjorie, Sophie and Abigail all look shocked and began to chatter amongst themselves.

Colin continued to scan the trees but after a minute assumed that the man was alone.

Bryn called out, "Cover me." She jumped over the fortified guardrail and bounded down the steep hill. When she reached the man's body, she stopped and listened. Believing she was safe, she immediately began searching his dead body for any clues that might tell them who he was and if he had anything to do with the gunfire from earlier. She discovered only the handheld radio, a semiautomatic pistol and a .22 caliber bolt-action rifle. He had no identification or anything that would give them any idea why he was spying on them. Satisfied with her search, Bryn came back to the group only to find them debating their next move.

"We can't leave, no, we can't," Becky declared.

"I'm with Becky," Katherine added.

"Me too," Abigail said.

"Leaving them behind was never part of the plan," Marjorie chimed in. Ever since she defied Frank earlier in the morning, she had felt empowered.

"This might be a first, but I agree with the ladies," Frank said.

Hearing the conversation and having her own opinion, Bryn said, "No one gets left behind, period."

"I'm sorry, but his wishes were specific. I was given two conditions for leaving, and hearing that skirmish in the woods and the man down there fulfills that requirement.

This is not up for debate; we need to start moving," Colin declared.

"No!" Becky said.

"Becky, I'm sorry, but this is not up for a vote," Colin said.

"You can't make us," Becky charged.

Feeling frustrated, Colin took his massive hand and rubbed his face. He looked at Becky, then went to each face in the group. He had to come up with some compromise, but what, he wasn't sure yet.

"You're outnumbered," Bryn said.

"Guys, listen. We've been lucky, but we can't sit here forever. We need to move on. What if that man was an advance or scout for whoever did all that shooting? Soon they'll be here, and we might not have enough to fight them off. Becky, you need to see this from Nicholas' prospective," Colin explained.

"You're asking me to agree to something I can never agree to. No, I will not pack up and head north."

"How about this? We keep a small team to go look, say…"

Bryn raised her hand and said, "Count me in."

"Me too," Rob said.

"I want to go," Abigail chirped.

"That's not going to happen," Colin said to Abigail.

"I agree, you're not going out there," Becky said to Abigail. She could see the anxiety in her, and the fear for her father was written into the deep wrinkles of her furrowed brow and pursed lips.

"Bryn and Rob will go. The rest of us will press

forward in the Suburban and trailer. We'll leave them the old car," Colin said.

"I can't agree to this," Becky said.

"Please listen, we're not safe sitting here anymore. We need to go, you need to go. There's nothing you can do, so why not be heading north at least," Colin explained. He was deeply frustrated and the conversation he was having was not a surprise. He knew this was going to happen and didn't have any ideas just how to handle it if they refused.

"I think Colin has a point," Frank said.

"We're not leaving Nic and Proctor," Becky said, shooting a harsh look at her father.

"His plan doesn't leave them; we send these two looking for them while we begin the last leg of our trip. Sitting here and waiting won't change the outcome of what those two find out there," Frank replied.

"Here's the deal, while you all sit and debate this, Rob and I are heading out," Bryn declared as she opened the back of the Suburban. She opened the back cargo space and began stuffing food, water and extra ammunition into a backpack.

Rob followed her lead and started doing the same thing. As he stuffed his pack, he hoped Abigail would come to him, but with each item he stuffed, his desire turned to disappointment as she stayed by Becky's side.

With her pack now on her back and Rob ready to march in search of Nicholas and Proctor, Bryn turned to the bickering group and said, "We're off."

Frank came up to her, dangled the keys to the Dodge Dart and said, "You'll be needing these."

"Thanks."

"And I removed the battery. It's stashed over near the highway sign," Frank said.

"Good thinking," Bryn said. She stuffed the keys in her pocket, gave the group a sloppy salute, headed down the embankment and disappeared into the woods, with Rob following just behind.

"You see, they're off to find them. Now can we get off this road, please?" Colin begged.

Katherine leaned into Becky and said, "I don't like saying this, but they have a legitimate point. Sitting here makes us vulnerable, and there's nothing we're going to accomplish by sitting here."

Becky chewed on her lip, her mind racing.

Marjorie then added, "I agree with Katherine. Now that we've sent some people to look for them, let's get off this road."

Becky turned to Abigail, took her hands and asked, "What do you think?"

"Just leaving feels wrong, but what I'm hearing makes sense, and if it's what Dad wishes, then we should go."

Becky turned to Colin and said, "We go, but not too far. Somewhere we can get off the road and hide."

Not wanting to debate anymore, Colin begrudgingly agreed, "Fine. Let's load up."

Vista, CA

Vincent took the earlier incident in stride and even found it humorous. Here he was, a big, bad Marine and he allowed himself to get held up by a woman and her child. At first, he did think that his time was up, but it took him only a few minutes to come to the conclusion she didn't want to kill him, but might if she felt threatened. He counted his lucky stars that the person who managed to catch him off guard wasn't a cold-blooded killer. Like he did most of his life, he never looked at the negative, he always found the lesson in anything, and this lesson stood out like a massive neon sign for him.

He had inspected the cabinet refrigerator they had raided, and noticed Noah had done as he was told and took every bottle and packet. The problem was he didn't know what he was grabbing, and they didn't get what they had come for. This made him wonder if they'd come back, probably not, he imagined, but nowadays he just couldn't be sure. When people were desperate, they were capable of desperate measures. Plus, she seemed very paranoid and she had to figure the odds of getting a jump on him again would be slight. However, he wasn't going to take any chances, so he barred the doors and nailed the windows shut.

He hadn't eaten yet today, and the hunger pangs were becoming stronger by the minute. He hurried to the kitchen and began to browse for food. He found a jar of crunchy peanut butter and an unopened jar of jelly. His mouth watered thinking about the combination. As he prepared a peanut butter and jelly sandwich with the last two slices of stale bread, which he toasted to make it more palatable, he caught a figure moving near the gate. He placed the butter knife down and stared, just waiting to see the movement again. It was like déjà vu for him.

The gate was two hundred feet from the main house, but after his experience, specifically with the mob, he knew someone could clear it and be at the house in less than a minute.

Without taking his eyes off the gate, he reached behind him and grabbed his rifle, which he'd laid on the center kitchen island.

A head appeared over the top of the gate, looked left and right and disappeared.

"Twice in one day, things are getting bad out there, I guess," he murmured to himself.

Again the head popped up, and with catlike reflexes, the person jumped over the gate.

A smile stretched across Vincent's face when he recognized that it was the boy, Noah.

Noah rushed towards the barn and disappeared.

"Going for the garage, are you?" Vincent said to himself, his smile still wide. He left the kitchen and made for the garage.

In the garage, Vincent found a chair and placed it in the shadowy corner opposite the exterior door and cabinets. He draped himself with a large moving blanket and just waited.

He heard the turning of the doorknob followed by a slight creak of the exterior door that came into the garage from outside. For a brief moment, the sunlight splashed into the garage as Noah slipped in and closed the door. He paused for a moment and looked at the door that led into the house. Seeing it was closed, he dashed over to the cabinet and tried to open it but found it locked. He looked around but saw nothing. On the opposite wall, a long built-in workbench spanned the length of the garage. Noah rushed over there and began to search for something that would help him break in. What he didn't notice was just six feet away in the dark corner, Vincent sat quietly watching him.

"Oh, c'mon," Noah lamented at not finding something.

Not able to contain himself any longer, Vincent said, "The keys would make it easier."

Noah screamed and scurried back away from the bench. "Don't hurt me."

Vincent stood with his rifle slung across his body, holding a single crutch in the other.

Noah kept taking small steps backwards away from Vincent. "Please don't hurt me."

"Did you come to find the medicine you thought you took?"

"Yes," Noah answered, his voice quivering.

Just behind him several small boxes sat in his way.

He took two more half steps away from Vincent and fell backwards over the boxes. He landed on his butt hard and yelped in pain and surprise.

Vincent approached, genuinely concerned for Noah.

"No, leave me alone."

Vincent stopped and said in a reassuring voice, "I won't hurt you. Trust me, I'm a Marine and I'm actually one of the good guys."

Noah held up his trembling hands and begged, "Please don't hurt me. I messed up. I got the wrong stuff and, um, my mom is so mad at me."

Vincent held up his hands, his palms out and replied, "Noah? It's Noah, right?"

Noah nodded.

"I won't hurt you, I promise. I was wondering if you or your mother would come back. And what do you know, here you are."

Noah scooted away and got back to his feet. He looked at Vincent; then out of the corner of his eye, he looked towards the exterior door.

"Go, you can run. I won't chase you or hurt you, but you'll just leave without the medicine you need. Or you can stay for a few minutes while I get you what you need."

"You promise?"

"Yeah, of course."

"You swear?"

"I already promised, but I'll swear too if that's necessary."

Noah looked at Vincent apprehensively, but didn't know what to do. He thought about making a run for it but was too frightened.

"Does your mother know you're here?" Vincent asked as he hobbled over to the exterior door and opened it.

Noah didn't answer.

Vincent stepped outside, turned and said, "Follow me."

Noah stood and took one cautious step after another until he was outside. He looked for Vincent but didn't see him. He knew all he had to do was turn left and he'd be within a quick dash towards the gate. He thought about making that left turn but stopped when Vincent called out.

"Do you want the medicine or not?" Vincent called out from around the other corner. He stood next to one of the SUVs, which was covered with a thick tan car cover.

Noah looked at Vincent but hesitated.

Seeing how scared Noah was, Vincent tried to reassure him that he was safe. "Noah, I won't hurt you, but if you feel nervous, I understand. How about this, I'll get the medicine and put it in the bag you brought? Just toss it over here."

Noah took off his pack and did as Vincent asked.

Vincent picked up the bag and laughed when he saw it was a superhero backpack. He imagined Noah wearing this to school or taking it with him on a sleepover at a friend's. It reminded him of a more innocent time. He found himself feeling bad for Noah and the question came to mind to ask him who was ill. "Can I ask who needs the antibiotics?"

Noah was still frozen to the spot just outside the garage door. He looked at Vincent with his sad green eyes and said, "My daddy needs it."

"Oh, I'm sorry to hear that," Vincent said, then pulled off the cover and unlocked the SUV. He made a mental note to temper his comments. He grabbed a box from the backseat and opened it.

"My daddy was shot."

Vincent stopped and wondered if he had been in the mob attack. He thought about what to ask but decided to just stay quiet.

"He, um, is in a bad way," Noah said sadly.

Vincent finished putting in the medicine and tossed the pack. "Everything your mother will need is in there. I even put in some prescription pain meds."

Noah snatched the pack and said, "Thanks." He looked, took a step away but stopped. He turned back around and said, "I have to go. I know my mom's looking for me." He then sprinted away.

Vincent couldn't help but wonder if Noah's dad had come to the property that day. Maybe that was why she didn't trust him, but her comments didn't make sense. She had clearly mentioned hating men. However Noah's father had been shot, it had been traumatic for the entire family. He hoped that what little help he gave would be enough, and if it wasn't, he couldn't imagine the pain of loss Noah would experience by losing his father. Vincent could feel his foot throbbing and the hunger pangs came back. He rested against the SUV and began to think about all the children out there who had suffered, who had witnessed such horrific things. For him he hadn't yet truly seen what had become of the world, but soon he'd be right in the middle.

Wellsville, Utah

Nicholas opened his eyes and found himself in a strange room. He looked to his right and saw a body draped with a white sheet; he looked to his left and saw a woman wearing medical scrubs. He opened his dry mouth and asked, "Please tell me you're here to help me?"

"Yes, we're here to help."

"Who's that?" he asked, motioning to the body next to him.

"Your colleague."

"He's dead, right?"

"Was he a friend?" she asked.

Nicholas nodded. He could tell he was on some type of narcotic by the way he felt. "Will I be okay?"

"I think so, but the doctor can answer all your questions. Let me go get her," she said and left the small room.

Nicholas looked again at the draped body and felt so sorry for Proctor and for his wife, Katherine. What a tragic mistake going out to help Luke. Even though he hadn't voted to authorize it, he found himself feeling guilty.

A tap on the door jolted him back from his remorse.

The door opened, but a woman didn't enter like he expected. Two men came in.

"We heard you were awake," the first man said. He was average height, his black short thinning hair was cut in the style of what Nicholas used to know as a flattop. The man had a burly deep voice, which Nicholas recognized as being the man who had spoken to him in the forest.

"Hi," Nicholas replied.

The man looked at the far bed, which housed Proctor's body, and said, "He had a weak pulse when we got him here, but he didn't make it. I'm sorry."

"He was alive out there?" Nicholas asked, surprised to hear this revelation.

"Yeah, we thought he was dead too, but he had a bit left in him. He had lost too much blood by the time we got him back, and well…you know the rest."

"Who are you?" Nicholas asked.

"My name is Brock, and this is my cousin Logan. We're scouts for the town of Wellsville. We had been tracking those savages who took you since they came through our town a few days back. They robbed a couple farms, took some food, and kidnapped those two kids."

"So it was just a coincidence you came upon us?" Nicholas asked, genuinely curious.

"We came across the Summers kid and his sister not a couple hours before we ambushed those guys. He told us where you might be," Logan replied. He was taller and leaner than his cousin and without a doubt the younger of the two. The family resemblance came from jet black hair and green eyes. His voice had a similar tone but slightly higher.

"Luke?" Nicholas muttered.

"Yeah, that's his name. Their parents reported them missing, so when we ran into him and he had word on those guys, we killed two birds with one stone," Logan said.

"Enough of what happened out there. We stopped by

to check on you and," Brock said but hesitated; he looked at Logan, smiled and continued, "we have a surprise for you."

"Guys, I'm very thankful for you saving me, but I need to get back to my group."

Logan stepped over to the gurney where Proctor's body rested, unlocked the wheels and with a heavy shove began to push it towards the door that Brock was now holding open.

"Where are you taking him?" Nicholas asked in a somber tone.

"Just down to the coroner's office at the end of the hall," Brock informed him.

"Take care of him. I need to take him back with me," Nicholas said with a concerned look.

"No need to worry," Brock said then left. He stuck his head back in and said, "I'll be right back with that surprise."

Nicholas exhaled deeply and laid his head back onto the thick pillow. He hated being there, and being wounded was just a plain inconvenience. Thoughts of Becky and Abigail filled his mind. He prayed they were safe and cursed the entire situation that had led to his being there.

The door opened slowly.

Nicholas didn't raise his head because he assumed it was Brock.

"Can this surprise just wait? I need to get the doc to check me out. I really need to go."

"And where would you be going?" Becky asked.

"Huh?" Nicolas blurted out. He shot his head up and saw Becky and Abigail standing there.

"Daddy," Abigail cried out as she rushed the bed and hugged him tightly.

"What, how? Don't hug me too hard, Abby, you might pop a stitch."

Becky hurried to his side, took his hand and held it firmly. She leaned over and gave him a kiss. Several tears streamed down her face and her breathing increased with each second she sat there looking at him. "I'm so sorry, I'm so, so sorry."

"How is it you're here?" Nicholas asked, unsure if he might be in a drug-induced hallucination.

"It's a long story, but after all the shooting and Bryn killing some guy in the woods, Colin told us we were leaving and that it was your instructions to do so. I didn't agree at first, but we couldn't just sit there, especially after that guy."

"Who was this person Bryn killed?" Nicholas asked.

"I don't know, must have been with those guys who had you and Proctor."

Nicholas now remembered Cam mentioning one of his men were watching the group.

"Katherine is a mess," Becky said.

"And Evelyn?" Nicholas asked, referring to Proctor's eighteen-month-old daughter.

"It's so sad, all of it. She'll never remember her father," Becky said.

"I understand what you're saying," Nicholas replied.

"Daddy, I was so scared," Abigail whimpered, her embrace unrelenting.

"It will take a lot to take your old man out." Nicholas

laughed. He continued, "How are you doing, though?" He caressed her hair.

"Better now," Abigail answered.

"How's everyone else?" Nicholas asked Becky.

"Frazzled."

"I bet. I'll be out of here soon and we'll be on our way."

"We can't leave until they come back," Becky said.

Nicholas raised his brows, curious as to who she was talking about.

She picked up on his facial expression and said, "Bryn and Rob."

"What about Bryn and Rob?" he asked.

"They went looking for you."

"I gave specific instructions that no one attempt to rescue us. I know I was very specific on that."

"It was a compromise."

Nicholas tossed the sheets off him and struggled to get up.

"What are you doing?" Becky asked.

With great difficulty he managed to sit up. He looked at her and replied, "I'm going to go find them."

CHAPTER TWO

"Old friends pass away, new friends appear. It is just like the days. An old day passes, a new day arrives. The important thing is to make it meaningful: a meaningful friend - or a meaningful day." – Dalia Lama

Undisclosed Bunker Facility, Superstition Mountains, East of Apache Junction, Arizona

Michael rose from his bed, excited to be free of the restraints and the drugs they had been giving him for pain. During the evening, he made his request and Karina had made it so. He wanted to move around and see exactly where he was.

"Just take it easy," Karina said nervously, her hands out ready to grab him if he fell.

"I'll be okay, being stuck in bed for God knows how long has made my legs feel weak," Michael said as he took his first step off the bed. When his bare foot hit the cool laminate floor, he stopped and allowed himself to truly feel the sensation. "Why exactly did you guys have me drugged?"

"Too long, but please believe me, it was Anatoly's idea," Karina replied.

Michael was now putting all his weight on his shaky

legs; he scooted several steps and stopped. Closing his eyes, he imagined his body was firmly planted to the ground. It was a mental exercise he had learned while training years ago. He took several more steps, this time steadier and faster. "I'm feeling pretty good, a bit achy and tight, but pretty good."

"I'm so happy to hear that," Karina gleefully said, lightly clapping her hands.

Michael spent the next few minutes strutting around the room. He swung his arms and stretched his back by touching his toes. "Feels good, really does."

Karina and Michael laughed and chatted casually. This made him feel at ease, and for the first time in a long time he forgot all the troubles from the past several weeks.

The door opened abruptly, startling them.

"Something funny?" Anatoly asked, stepping into the room.

Michael froze at the sight of Anatoly. The carefree feelings he had were swept away in an instant upon his entrance.

"We're just celebrating Michael's full recovery. Look, Anatoly, he's walking around," Karina replied.

By her demeanor and tense response to Anatoly, Michael could tell they weren't exactly equals and that she was wary of him.

"Good, that means he's ready to talk," Anatoly said.

Michael asked, "What would you like to know?"

"The coordinates."

"Coordinates?" Michael asked. He truly didn't know what coordinates he was asking about, but deep down

Michael did know he knew something.

Anatoly looked at Karina and asked something in Russian.

"Please speak English," Michael requested.

"Listen, Michael, we need those coordinates, and you're the only person that has them. We can play games, or we can take this further," Anatoly threatened.

"What's he talking about?" Michael asked Karina.

"Anatoly, give me a moment, this is all too much for him," Karina stressed.

"A moment, we've given him weeks. We don't have time for this," Anatoly exclaimed just below a scream.

"Michael, please think. What do you remember, specifically what do you remember about your time with the CIA?"

Michael exhaled heavily and answered, "It's taken me a while to remember my life before. I recall being in the Army and even being in the CIA, but what I was doing on that ship is still unclear. I can remember your face, our time together before all of this. I even remember another Russian; I believe his name is Viktor. He was on that ship and he threatened to harm you if I didn't help. He was torturing me, I remember that. So this Viktor also wants the coordinates?"

"So you remember nothing specific?" Karina asked.

"I've had a rough several weeks," Michael joked.

Anatoly gave Michael a scowl.

"Are you guys CIA? Is this a CIA facility?" Michael asked.

"Do we look CIA?" Anatoly laughed.

"Actually, yeah, you could be, I at least know that."

"He's lying. We need to take this further."

"You tried the serums, but nothing worked. If he knew, then he would have told you," Karina reminded Anatoly of the drugs they had used on Michael to get him to speak. This was the real reason he had been lost in a fog since his arrival there.

"You drugged me to talk?" Michael asked.

Karina and Anatoly cross-talked.

Michael began to feel like he was having an out-of-body experience. He wasn't in control and needed to be. Frustrated himself by their lack of forthcoming, he exploded, "I will fully cooperate, but you need to be honest with me and start doing it now!"

They both stopped talking and looked at him.

"Who are you, where am I, and how do I know you?" he yelled.

Karina spoke first. "We're your friends."

"That's not enough, I need specifics. And let me give you a 411, friends don't drug each other," he snapped.

"Walk with me, Michael," Anatoly said, his tone measured. "Let me explain everything to you."

Vista, CA

Vincent sat drinking his morning coffee and looking at his bandaged foot. He had never asked why his former hosts hadn't put a cast on it but could only guess it was because they didn't have one. He hated to have to deal with the injury, but he still counted his blessings daily. Never had he heard of someone falling from a chopper and living, better to have his foot broken instead of something worse, like his back or, even worse, he could have lost his life.

This morning he decided not to make his morning jaunt to the top of the avocado grove. According to his own schedule, he was just days from leaving and heading north, and if someone was going to come inside again, he didn't want to possibly injure himself coming down to stop them. Taking a perch in the upstairs guest bedroom, he had a full view of the front drive, gate and road beyond.

Occasionally, a car or truck would drive by, all were older model vehicles. How Roger had managed to have a later model SUV operational was a miracle but not surprising for someone of his talent. The entire situation was so odd, like a one-in-a-billion situation. He had fallen from a helicopter, been rescued and received care from one of the richest men in the United States, who then gave him two life-altering choices, either take a seat in his secure bunker, or have more than enough equipment and resources to help him on his journey back to Idaho. It was all of it that made Vincent feel his survival to this moment wasn't pure chance but divine. God had a plan for him; he just didn't know what it was yet.

Vincent hadn't practiced religion since he was a teenager. He had grown up Catholic and found the services boring, mundane and too ritualistic for his liking. While in the Marine Corps, he drifted further away from God. The experiences he had while in took him in the opposite direction as some of his comrades. Seeing such horror drove some men to embrace religion and God, but for him he looked at all of it and questioned what kind of God would allow such things to happen. When he had heard about the EMP attack, it again confirmed his newfound belief that there was no God, then the miraculous fall and rescue. He at first had tried to brush it off, but it was just all too perfect to be a coincidence. However, he was struggling to make sense of a God that allowed such barbarism then intervened in his personal survival.

He took a large sip of the hot coffee and smiled. Soon he wouldn't be able to enjoy his coffee like this. On the road, he'd have to feed his addiction, and yes, for him it was an addiction. Even a day without coffee would bring on a raging migraine headache that many over-the-counter pain medicines couldn't relieve.

The morning clouds from the coastal marine layer hung low, blocking out the sun. Seeing an early morning blue sky in Southern California was easily a fifty-fifty proposition, unlike Idaho, where the bluebird mornings were common unless a storm system was moving in.

His thoughts drifted to Noah. He hoped the boy hadn't gotten into too much trouble and that his mother would take it easy on him. He also hoped the medicines he gave him would be helpful.

A loud banging at the gate surprised him. He had been lost in thought and hadn't seen anyone walking up.

"Well, good morning. Who's out there?" Vincent asked out loud. He couldn't see who was there, but someone was, as they banged loudly on the gate again.

"Open up!" a woman's voice cried out.

Vincent stood quickly, spilling his coffee. He slung his rifle and grabbed his crutches.

"Open up!" the woman again cried out.

Vincent opened the front door slightly and peered out. The last thing he wanted was to walk into an ambush.

"Please, open up!" the woman yelled, her voice now sounding distressed.

"Who are you?" Vincent hollered back.

"Bridgette!"

"Who?"

No reply came back for a few seconds; then the woman said, "Nunea!"

Vincent wasn't expecting her but could only imagine it had something to do with Noah and the medicine. He stepped outside the house and hobbled over to the stairs then stopped. The thought entered his mind that she might try to rob him again or do something stupid. "What do you want?"

Seconds again passed without a reply; she then answered, "I need your help."

"You're not going to shoot at me or something, are you?"

"No, please. My husband, he's taken a turn for the worse."

Vincent cleared the stairs and started for the gate. The strong aroma of sage brush hit him; it was a smell that reminded him instantly of life at Camp Pendleton. The idea that she might do something wasn't far from his mind, but what possibly could she want now, he told himself as he stopped ten feet from the gate and placed his right hand on the back strap of his pistol holstered on his tactical vest. "What's up?"

"You said you knew first aid. I need your help."

"Why should I help you anymore? You stuck a pistol in my face and threatened to shoot me and, oh, that was just yesterday," Vincent mocked. A desire not to help her rose in his mind, but he quickly dismissed it. He was a Marine and considered himself a good person. He thought about the inner conversation he had just had minutes before, and maybe his new mission in life, maybe his reason for living was so he could help others.

"I'm sorry, but you don't know what we've gone through. Can you help or not?" she begged.

"Where was he shot?" Vincent asked, remembering what Noah had told him.

"In his stomach, but it's festering."

Vincent couldn't imagine she was setting him up, but he wasn't about to go blindly. "Give me a few minutes. I'll be right back." He hobbled off.

Like he promised, he returned a few minutes later but behind the wheel of the SUV. He unlocked the gate and pushed the heavy gate open.

She stood just on the other side, waiting patiently. However, she wasn't the woman he had encountered yesterday. She looked tired, stressed and her clothes were stained with blood.

He was bringing everything with him. Yes, it was risky,

but leaving it behind unattended was even riskier. Just as he was getting in, he said, "Get in."

Bridgette quickly got in. She watched as Vincent awkwardly got back in the cab. He tossed his crutches and rifle in the backseat and slammed the door. Before he engaged the transmission, he looked at her and said, "No funny business, you understand?"

"Listen, I'm sorry about yesterday. I'm desperate, please understand," she answered, her tone conciliatory.

"Fair enough," he said as he put the vehicle into gear and sped off.

Wellsville, Utah

Becky could tell by the look on Nicholas' face that he wasn't listening to the doctor's recommendations.

And she was right; Nicholas looked past the doctor towards the window and the trees beyond that.

No one had any reports on Bryn and Rob, and this unnerved Nicholas. He was already filled with guilt over Proctor; now he was faced with possibly losing two others in his group. He and Becky had sat up talking last night about the entire situation, and she now agreed that the idea of having a democracy was just plain silly. It sounded practical before they left, but that was their pre-apocalypse mindset. Few people had ever lived in such situations and thought that a simple vote could make everything all right. But the vast majority of people lacked real experience of combat and warlike situations. What was best was one person making the tough calls. Nicholas mainly faulted himself. He had some combat experience, but it had been over two decades before, and in many ways he had become soft. He'd allowed himself to be talked out of what he knew was the right call. The consensus he and Becky had come to last night was that he would be in total control. They'd keep their little democracy but only for decisions that were considered minor.

"Mr. McNeil, are you listening to me?" the doctor asked. She could clearly see he wasn't focused on her.

"Um, yeah. You recommend I take it easy."

"Mr. McNeil, you have been shot. Fortunately the bullet traveled clean through; however, you could still open yourself up for infection. Your number seven and eight ribs on your right side are bruised and you sustained a concussion."

"Got it."

Becky thought about asking Nicholas to take the doctor's words more seriously, but she knew him and it was a waste of breath.

The doctor frowned, and her irritation with his lack of respect for her was apparent. "Here is some Advil, some Cephalexin to prevent infection, and if the pain is more than the Advil can handle, here's some hydrocodone."

Becky took the three bottles and tossed them in a small satchel.

Still ignoring the doctor, Nicholas turned and asked Becky, "Where's Abby?"

"Out front with Colin and the others."

"And Katherine?"

"She's out there too. I forgot to mention she wants to hold a funeral here in two days."

Nicholas nodded.

"The nurse will check you out," the doctor said and exited the room.

As soon as the door to his room closed, Nicholas exclaimed, "Thank God. Can we get the hell out of here?"

"Be grateful, these people have been generous and very nice."

He thought for a second and agreed, "Don't get me wrong, this has been a miracle. I could never have imagined a town would still function and operate almost like nothing had happened here."

Becky stayed with Nicholas as he went through the procedural checking out from the clinic. After a few jokes and some heavy exhaling from Nicholas, as the process took longer than he wanted, they found themselves outside.

When Nicholas saw Colin and the group, he jumped out of the wheelchair and headed towards them. "Colin, we need to have a few words."

Colin didn't have to guess what it was about. "Yes, boss."

Nicholas opened his arms and said, "C'mon here, buddy."

Colin looked at him strangely, not expecting a warm reunion. He embraced Nicholas and said, "Glad you're okay."

"And please, stop calling me *boss*. I've already asked you before to stop that. Please, enough."

"It's a Southern thing."

"Well, we're not in the South, nor are we anywhere close to the Mason-Dixon Line."

"Roger that, I'll stop."

"Did you do as I asked?" Nicholas queried.

"Yep, we're to see him as soon as you're ready," Colin answered, referring to the mayor of Wellsville.

"Good," Nicholas said as he went for his watch but couldn't find it. He turned to Becky and asked, "Where's my watch?"

She held up the shimmering gold piece and replied, "Right here." She walked over and handed it to him. "It was one of the first things I checked on after I saw you yesterday."

Nicholas took the timepiece in his hand and stared at it. This watch meant a lot to him. It very well could be the last item he'd have from his brother, Michael. His mind raced to where he might be and if he was okay; then he remembered it was Michael McNeil he was worried about and that he shouldn't be. From his earliest recollections, Michael was a tough and able person. He had been a great older brother and always looked out for him when he was a child. He had been hard on Nicholas but had good reason. Nicholas respected and loved his brother and wished he could be there with him as they went through this struggle. Unsure of where he was or if he'd see him again, this watch represented Michael and their brotherly love. It was one of the few prized possessions he had.

"I forgot to mention, the mayor wants to see you too, so it wasn't too hard to get this meeting," Colin informed Nicholas.

"Good, let's not keep the mayor waiting," Nicholas said, putting his attention back on where he was. He pocketed the watch and climbed into the Suburban.

Undisclosed Bunker Facility, Superstition Mountains, East of Apache Junction, Arizona

Michael looked around the room. It was just like his hospital room and the seemingly endless hallways, stark white with no windows. He longed to see the sun and to breathe fresh air.

Anatoly didn't share anything significant along their way to this new room. He did tell Michael he was in a bunker in the Arizona Mountains and that he had never been there before but knew about its existence. He opened up that they were not CIA but that Michael definitely was and had joined their cause against Viktor. However, what he didn't discuss was what the end game was. And finally, what were the coordinates for?

"Take a seat, Michael," Anatoly instructed.

Michael did as he asked. It felt good to sit, but he couldn't relax.

Karina walked in then and closed the door.

Michael took note along his walk that he didn't see anyone else. The only people he had seen since being at the bunker was Anatoly, Karina and the nurse. The bunker felt large, but it seemed empty.

Karina took a seat next to Michael and placed a large file in front of him. "This might help jog your memory."

Michael went to open up the file but stopped when Anatoly spoke. "Before you do that, let's get to the heart of the matter. I have to admit that I thought you were lying about your memory loss, but it appears you have truly suffered from your injuries. Our doctors tell us that your memory will come back. The issue we have is limited time, and if we fail, the world will be lost."

Michael cracked a smile and joked, "I think the world is already lost."

Anatoly ignored him and continued, "Viktor is part of a group that is bent on world domination, and the only way he believes he can do that is by being in possession of what you'll see in that folder."

Michael again went to open it but was stopped once more.

"Before you open it, I want to impress upon you that with your memory loss, what you're about to see and hear will confuse you. You might even think we're crazy, but I can assure you that the Michael we knew before was fully committed to our task."

"Anatoly, I wish I could remember what this is all about," Michael replied. He turned to Karina and said, "And I wish I could remember us, I do vaguely and I know we had something, but it's the strangest thing to have bits of memory but also feel I'm looking at a stranger." Michael looked back at Anatoly and continued, "Whatever you're about to share with me, I will listen and I pray it will bring the man I was back. You said there isn't time to waste, so let's do this."

Anatoly was about to speak but Michael interrupted. "And please don't drug me again. I'm here and I want to help," he said, but in his heart he was still wary, and as his memory returned, he would be open with prejudice.

What Michael said made Anatoly crack a smile, which was unusual for him. "Viktor is the head of a group called the Union of Salvation. They were a defunct group that had been instrumental in Russian politics and affairs for over two hundred years. In fact, some claim they were the ones who sowed the seeds of revolution before the Bolsheviks. They now have been resurrected by Viktor and their aims are greater. They wish to dominate the world and create some sort of utopia. The problem we have is their utopian visions require a drastic reduction in the world's population. What you've seen happen has been all of their making, but they feel in order to control the world, they need one item, and this is where you come in. Open the folder."

Michael did and the first thing he discovered was group of photographs, most of them old. He picked them up and began to shuffle through them.

Anatoly remained quiet and watched him process the images.

"These aren't stirring anything in my mind. Um, this thing Viktor is after, it looks like a relic. What is it?"

Anatoly frowned at Karina and answered, "That, my friend, is the Spear of Destiny. It goes by other names like the Holy Lance, the Holy Spear, the Lance of Longinus or the Spear of Longinus, but fact is, those photos are of a replica that is housed in Austria."

"I'm sorry, I don't recall any of this," Michael lamented.

"It will come back," Karina said as she touched his leg.

"What is it?"

"The Spear of Destiny is the name given to the lance that pierced the side of Jesus as he hung on the cross."

"I really hate that I don't recall this, but it does seem familiar. I don't understand; why would Viktor and his Union of Salvation want a relic?"

Karina stepped in and answered, "Because it holds powers. Those who are in possession of the spear will have total power and be able to control their destinies."

"I'm sorry, but this is a joke, right?" Michael asked.

"No, Michael it's not a joke, it's very real. Many have sought after its power and many have held it in their hands. Men like Constantine, Charlemagne, Frederick Barbarossa the First, Herod the Great, Maurice the Manichean, Theodosius, Alaric, Theodoric, Justinian, Charles Martel, Heinrich the First, and Adolf Hitler."

Michael was feeling a bit overwhelmed by the story and was beginning to wonder if Anatoly and Karina were crazy and members of the tinfoil-hat club. He then began to become concerned about his own sanity, as apparently he believed in this. He then looked at the world around him and decided that it couldn't be any crazier than what was happening to everything.

"I do know how hearing this sounds, but you hold the key to all of it," Anatoly flatly said.

"The coordinates?"

"Yes, Michael, you are the only living person who knows the whereabouts of this powerful relic."

Michael looked at both of them and asked, "How is it that I'm the only person?"

Anatoly looked at Karina and said, "Tell him."

"You have nothing to fear, trust me."

"Tell me."

"We had them all killed. You, however, did something that no one else had done before. You had it inscribed on something, and only you know where that item is."

"How is it that I'm a party to this whole thing? I'm a CIA agent."

"Michael, you're much more than that, my friend, much more."

Vista, CA

The first thing that hit Vincent was the smell of what could only be described as *death*. He'd encountered the smell before in hospitals and overseas in triage facilities. Then he saw Bridgette's husband, Ron. He wasn't sure if the smell added to the overall feel, but once he laid eyes on him, all Vincent could think was that he was looking at a dead man.

Ron was covered in a sticky sweat that clung to his ashen skin. The pajamas he was wearing were soiled with blood, vomit and old sweat. The bedroom itself was large and beautifully decorated. Vincent could tell at one time they had money and spent it on lavish furnishings. He couldn't tell if they were ever neat and orderly people, but they definitely weren't now. A large pile of soiled sheets sat in the far corner, but the floor was relatively free of debris as if someone was attempting to maintain some cleanliness. A large, eight-foot-tall set of French doors sat opposite the king-sized master bed and were open to allow fresh air to come in, but even with that the smell was intense.

Bridgette hurried to Ron's side and took his hand. He was shaking from what was most likely a fever brought on by infection. The severity of the fever was so high he could barely open his eyes to acknowledge her presence.

Upon entering the house and making his way to the upstairs bedroom, Vincent took notice that Noah was nowhere to be seen. This didn't alarm him, as the house was large, but he made a mental note.

"Honey, I have a man here that might be able to help," Bridgette said to Ron in a whisper.

Ron didn't open his eyes, but he did hear her. He opened his mouth and unintelligible sounds came out.

She turned to Vincent, who was still standing in shock at the scene in front of him. He didn't know what he could do. During his time in the Marine Corps he'd had advanced first-aid training, but Ron's condition was past his skill set.

"Can you help him?"

"I, ah, I can see what is wrong," Vincent said as he hobbled over next to her.

"His wound has become very infected, see," she said, lifting up his pajama top to show a blackened hole in his lower abdomen. His belly had swollen in the area surrounding the wound, with reddish string-like tentacles coming from it. "He went into the half-conscious state last night."

Vincent leaned over to get a better look and said, "It's obviously infected. Um, what was he shot with?"

"A handgun."

Vincent searched his mind for questions that might help. "Did the bullet pass through?"

"No, it's still in there."

"The bullet is still in there?" Vincent asked, astonished by this and factored that this could have helped create the environment for the infection to take hold.

"You have to get it out," Vincent said with urgency.

"I thought about that, but I don't know how to perform surgery. I tried to find a doctor at the hospital and—" she said but purposely cut herself off.

Vincent could tell there was more to the hospital story but didn't want to explore it just yet. He wondered if he could perform the surgery.

She looked up at him, tears forming in her green eyes, and asked, "Can you do it? Please save him."

"I'm not a surgeon, I know first aid, but—" he replied but was interrupted.

"Please."

"Please, mister, help us," Noah said from the doorway.

Vincent looked at him and didn't know how he could say no. He just needed to feel confident that if he failed, they wouldn't hold it against him. "I'll try to remove it, but..." He stopped short of saying it in front of Noah. "Can we talk in private?"

She nodded and took him to a large walk-in closet.

He closed the door and said, "Listen, I'm not a doctor. I just want to make myself clear on this. I'll go in and remove the bullet and do what I can, but I want to make it very clear that I don't know what I'm doing."

"I understand."

Vincent's breathing had increased and he became blunt, "I could kill him."

"If I do nothing, he's going to die anyway, I fear, and if this helps save him, then I have to risk it."

He could see the pain in her eyes, and again this might be his new mission. "I'll do it."

Wellsville, Utah

The short drive from the clinic to the city offices was pleasant, and if you had just been plopped down without any knowledge, you'd think the world was the same.

Nicholas marveled at how everything seemed so *normal*. People walked with strollers down the streets, and in the park across from the city offices, children played. He found it all so odd and in some ways unsettling. He asked himself how this little place had become an oasis in the madness that had taken over the world. He planned on asking the question, because from appearances, they had done something he hadn't seen in any municipality or urban center since leaving San Diego.

When they stopped in front of the small single-level

building that fronted the appropriately named Main Street, several armed men stepped out and met them.

Nicholas recognized one of them as Brock. "Hi, Brock, good to see you."

"Same, Mr. McNeil."

"Just call me Nic. I'm sure this is a stupid question, but no reports from your patrols about my two friends?"

"No, sir. Right this way," Brock said, motioning towards the front doors.

Inside, Nicholas found it exactly how he'd imagined it would look. The floors were covered in a worn carpet. The walls were painted a neutral tan and adorned with framed images and paintings of mountain landscapes. Above him, a white drop ceiling made him feel a bit crowded as the height was just shy of eight feet.

Brock took him down the hall and into a large boardroom. The far walls had windows that spanned the length, but the light of day was blocked with thick metal blinds.

Seated at the long twenty-foot wood-laminate table were seven people, five men and two women, all white. All were middle-aged except for one man and one woman.

The man at the far head of the table motioned him to come in further and said, "Welcome, welcome to Wellsville." He was average height, older, balding, and was seated in a wheelchair.

"Hi," Nicholas replied as he slowly stepped into the room. He could feel pain emanating from his side and then remembered that he hadn't taken any pain medication.

At Nicholas' request, Colin joined him. When Colin's

THE DEFIANT: AN UNBEATEN PATH

towering stature entered the room, Nicholas noticed several people react. He imagined they weren't used to seeing such a large black man in this part of the world. He remembered the demographics for small mountain towns were primarily white, to the point of being almost homogeneous.

"My name is Nicholas McNeil, and this is my friend and partner, Colin Somerville."

Colin grinned with his typical toothy grin and waved. "Hi, ya'll."

"Please, gentlemen, take a seat," the man in the wheelchair said. Right after Nicholas and Colin sat, the man introduced himself, "My name is Chad Smith, I'm the mayor of Wellsville, and to my right is Sally Braithwaite, my secretary, going down and around we have Deborah Shumway, John Christiansen, Thomas Fielding, Jason Bagley and Chuck Summers. They are the council people of our great town."

"Nice to meet you. I want to first thank you for saving my life. I have to admit your generosity and hospitality was welcome and unexpected."

"Unexpected?" Chad asked.

Nicholas looked at Colin, then answered, "Yes, every town we've encountered has been either a threat because they've collapsed into mob rule, or we were turned away with the threat of violence if we came anywhere near it."

"I'm sorry to hear that so many towns and cities haven't been able to manage this crisis," Chad lamented.

"From what I've seen, you have something special, and while I thank you, I'd suggest you need to be more careful who you allow in here. Not everyone will be as nice as we are."

"We have turned our fair share away. Let's just say we profile who comes through, and we do monitor their presence while they are here. We trust to a degree then verify. We're nice but not fools, Mr. McNeil."

"I wasn't saying you were fools."

"I know, so let's talk about why we wanted to see you. I know Brock told you we also wanted to talk with you."

"Yes," Nicholas replied. He wanted to get to the topic of what he wanted to ask but found himself obligated to let Chad speak first.

"A thriving town can only remain so if it has rules or laws. It must be administered fairly within the rule of law by an executive and an elected body of the citizenry. That's the first component; secondly, it must have able-bodied citizens who work actively on its behalf. It is this second half that is why I have asked to speak with you. You see, we have lost people, a large number have left, others have died and some have been killed. In order for us to a have a thriving and functional city, we must have people. We have a small population. Before the war we had about thirty-five hundred people, we're now down to half that. Our council has adapted to this crisis by having the town pull together. As a people we've always been prepared for such emergencies, but we believe this crisis won't be fixed for a very long time if at all. Because of our belief that this crisis won't end anytime soon, we immediately went to work creating an infrastructure for our town's survival, but those plans and that infrastructure requires manpower," Chad said and cleared his throat, he then continued. "I'll be blunt,

Mr. McNeil; we'd like you and your group to stay. I don't know what your plans were or where you were headed, but we can offer a stable and safe environment."

Nicholas was floored by the proposition. It came at him out of left field, but it stirred something in him. He looked at Colin, whose only response was a raised eyebrow. He thought for a few seconds and replied, "Mr. Mayor, I don't know how to respond. I wasn't expecting you to say this. In fact, I had no idea what you'd ask of us."

"What does your gut say? I'm a believer in following your instincts," Chad said.

"To be quite frank, I like the idea, but I also have a skeptical side to me that says, no, do your due diligence. We've been through a lot to get here, and like I mentioned earlier, the world has really gotten bad."

"I can assure you, if we were bad people up to nefarious things, we wouldn't have allowed you here much less given you the care you've just experienced."

Nicholas nodded after Chad said that. It didn't make sense for people to save you and care for you with the eventual goal of killing you. "I have to say, I'm intrigued by the offer, but I can't make this decision myself. It wouldn't be fair."

"You sure you don't want to? Look what happened last time you put it to a vote," Colin said half-jokingly, reminding him of the fateful decision that found them now in Wellsville.

Nicholas glared at Colin and put his attention back on Chad. "I really need to ask my group, so I hope you don't need my decision right this second."

"No, please take some time to think about it and discuss it with your people. I also understand that two in your group are missing," Chad said.

"Correct, that's why I wanted to talk with you. I'd like request some help looking for them, if you could spare some people."

"I already instructed Brock to do whatever was necessary to locate them. Brock is the head of our security patrols. He's doubled them and had them searching."

Again Nicholas found himself shocked. *Is there no end to these people's kindness?* he thought. "You are on top of everything here. Very impressive."

"It's our responsibility to help one another, even strangers."

"I have another request. One in our group was killed. We'd like your permission to bury him here."

"Of course," Chad said. He looked at Sally and continued, "Sally, take care of the arrangements and make sure there are flowers." He looked back at Nicholas and offered, "Do you need a clergyman to officiate a religious service?"

"Let me check."

"One last item, where can we park our trailer and camp?" Nicholas asked.

"No need to camp, I've arranged for several vacant houses to be made available for your stay. No need to be roughing it," Chad replied, smiling.

"Um, that's not necessary."

"Why would you want to sleep on the ground? Just use a few houses; your back will thank me."

"Fine, we'll do that."

"Good, Brock will take you to them. Take care, Mr. McNeil, and nice meeting you, Mr. Somerville, and please seriously consider our offer."

"I'll say goodbye, then. I'll get back to you soon about our decision on your generous offer," Nicholas said as he stood.

Brock escorted them back to the Suburban.

When the door closed and they had their privacy, Colin asked, "Whatcha think?"

"Not sure. My gut says, wow, what a nice place. I mean, look, fucking kids are over there jumping and playing, but my head says this is too good to be true."

"Which you going with?" Colin asked.

"A combination of both."

Vista, CA

Vincent looked at his blood-covered hands, then to Ron's body below him. The four-inch incision he had made on his lower abdomen was seeping blood and thick pus. There was no doubt the second he opened Ron that he had an infection, but the infection was far worse than he had imagined, and it even appeared that some of his tissue surrounding the wound and much more internally had begun to decay, meaning that gangrene might have set in. There were so many reasons why Ron didn't survive the surgery, but his ultimate prognosis hadn't been good regardless. Vincent thought that more than likely he had also developed sepsis, a fatal blood infection if left untreated. The trauma Vincent was feeling was nothing in comparison to what Bridgette or Noah were experiencing.

The scene was bloody and gruesome but made worse with Bridgette's wailing grief. She sat next to Ron's body and held his lifeless hand.

Noah stood next to her. Tears of pain and loss streamed down his innocent face and dripped from his chin.

There were no words to describe this scene except tragic.

Vincent finally spoke. "I'm so sorry. I am so very sorry."

Bridgette wailed.

Noah looked at Vincent, but his quivering lips didn't mutter a word.

Vincent felt uncomfortable and in some ways like an intruder on a very private moment. He stood up and went to the bathroom. He turned the handle and was surprised to see water pour from the rubbed bronze faucet. He washed the thickening blood from his hands with cold water and toweled off.

Bridgette's wails continued to echo off the walls and tile floors.

He walked back into the bedroom and found them exactly where he had left them. He contemplated trying to comfort her but then dissuaded himself, thinking that was inappropriate. The Marines had taught him a lot, but failed to give him instruction on how to handle these types of situations.

"I'm going to step out for a bit. Let me know if I can help with, um," he said but cut himself short because the next word was *body*. It just all sounded too morbid. He turned the knob on the door when Bridgette cried out.

"Don't go, please."

"I can stay."

"If you need to step out, I understand, but don't leave, stay," she said, looking up at him. Her eyes were swollen with tears, and snot hung from her dripping nose.

"I'm going to step out, but I'll stay. I won't leave you, I promise," he said and deeply meant it. "I'm sorry, I really am."

"You did nothing wrong. It's this fucking world!" she suddenly screamed, her anger stemming from a deep emotional loss.

"I'll be downstairs if you need me," Vincent said and left. When he closed the door, he rested his weight against it and sighed. He looked up and out loud said, "I guess I was wrong, God, you didn't keep me alive to save lives."

CHAPTER THREE

"Every person has free choice. Free to obey or disobey the Natural Laws. Your choice determines the consequences. Nobody ever did, or ever will, escape the consequences of his choices." – Alfred A. Montapert

Wellsville, Utah

The morning sun slowly crept into the kitchen of the little house Nicholas and the group were using. The sun's rays found Nicholas perched on a stool, looking out the window.

His group had voted to stay but only until they found Bryn and Rob. They'd then take another vote. They thought this the prudent route. Like Nicholas, they were all excited about the prospect of what Wellsville could be but, like Nicholas, wanted to ensure it was the right move. Nicholas had given the analogy that this was their first date with Wellsville, and you don't really know someone on a first date.

Their cautious approach also had them all unanimously vote to stay in the same house. Together they were harder to kill was the consensus.

The night was broken into shifts, and Nicholas had taken the early morning shift against Becky's objections. He might be healing, but he felt he still needed to pull his own weight.

Soft footsteps behind him in the kitchen caused him to turn. There he found Sophie.

She wiped sleep from her eyes and sauntered to the pantry.

"Good morning," Nicholas said.

Sophie was not a morning person and it showed in her response. "Morning." She stretched and yawned heavily.

As she scoured the pantry for what foods had been deposited for them from the townspeople, he said, "Sophie, I just want you to know that we're not leaving until we find Bryn."

"I know."

"I won't go anywhere until we have found her."

"I know," she again said, not looking at him as she pulled a box of crackers from a shelf.

"I just wanted to tell you that it's a priority of mine."

"I know."

Nicholas chuckled and said, "You're talkative, aren't you?"

She came out of the pantry, her lips smacking as she chewed on crackers and replied, "Nic, you're a good guy. I know you won't leave her."

"I'm glad you know."

She stuffed a couple more crackers in her mouth and said, "Not only do I know you'll never leave her, she knows. That's the most important thing."

"But she doesn't know we're even here."

"Precisely, she will never abandon you because she

knows in her heart you'd never abandon her. You see, my sister has her faults, but once you get into her heart, she'll never give up on you, never. That is an admirable trait and one you two share."

"Hmm." Nicholas shrugged. It was nice hearing her say what she said, and he did feel that way about all of them. They had in a short time become his extended family, and Nic would do anything for family. It was built into his DNA.

"Nice talk, I'm going to go lie back down," Sophie said and left.

Nicholas smiled as he watched her leave. He turned back around and looked through the grime-covered window. Far beyond to the southwest he saw the hills where he'd been held and wondered if Bryn and Rob were out there somewhere. He prayed they were still alive and only lost, or maybe, knowing Bryn, she was too skeptical to come into town. Their experiences had left them all guarded, but Bryn was on high alert and her level of trust was minimal.

"Where are you, Bryn? Where are you?"

Vista, CA

Vincent's slowly opened his eyes to find Noah standing above him, causing him to jump. "You scared me."

"Sorry."

"Is everything all right?" Vincent asked and pulled

himself up to a seated position. He had spent the night at their house and found the living room couch an acceptable but not perfect alternative to the bed he had at the compound. Leaving the compound unattended made him nervous, but he'd left nothing there that he needed for his cross-country trip. That was all in the SUV, and he made sure he parked that in her garage.

"Everything is fine. You were just snoring loud."

"Did you wake me?"

"Yes."

"Hmm," Vincent grunted and stood. He walked to the large bay window and looked out. The view from this window gave him a clear and unfettered perspective of the long driveway and main road. He didn't have a view of his compound but could see the avocado grove in the distance.

Bridgette's house sat upon large acreage too, as most did in the general vicinity. This gave him a general sense of ease and reduced the number of scavengers he'd have to deal with.

"How's your mother?" Vincent asked.

"She's lying upstairs next to dad," Noah answered with a somber tone.

Vincent turned and said, "I can't say enough how sorry I am."

"It's okay, I mean, I'll miss my dad, but Mom said he was probably going to die anyway."

Vincent didn't know how to follow up on that, so he left it alone, but he did want to know how he came to get shot. "What happened?"

"Some people came. My dad fought with them; they

shot him."

"What happened after that?"

"They ran off with a bunch of food and stuff."

"What did your mom do?"

"She was hiding with me."

"So they came up and just shot him?"

"Not sure, they were just talking when suddenly it turned into a fight. There were three of them. My mom took me to their bedroom to hide in the closet. We heard them fighting; then a gun went off. We were too afraid to leave the closet. When we thought it was safe, we found him outside."

"Didn't your dad have a weapon?"

"My dad had a bat."

"What about the pistol your mom has, the one she shot at me with?"

"She found that at the Taylor house next door when we went to look for medicine," Noah explained.

"So your dad was defenseless?"

"Dad says guns kill."

"They do, you just don't want to be the one dying," Vincent cracked then shrugged his shoulders in disappointment. He could never imagine not having the tools available to protect himself or his family if he had one. He resisted the urge to ask Noah more questions, and what was the point, he asked himself. The fact was right there and didn't need to be pressed anymore, especially to a child.

Noah gave a painful look and asked, "Are you going to leave us now?"

"I'll hang out and help with your dad, you know, bury

him."

"After that?"

"Do you have any relatives, grandparents, someone you can go to?"

"Yes, but they're far away."

"Where are they?"

"They live in Oklahoma. Granddad is a politician."

This tugged at Vincent's sense of duty to those in need. Immediately he began to question what he should do. In life it was always easier to know people were alone or vulnerable and do nothing, but the moment it becomes personal you feel an obligation.

"Did you wake him up after I told you not to," Bridgette snapped, admonishing Noah.

"I didn't mean to," Noah whimpered.

"It's okay. I needed to get up," Vincent said, coming to Noah's defense. He could see Bridgette was tired, strung out and no doubt in an emotionally unstable condition.

"It's not okay. He needs to do what I tell him to," Bridgette bellowed.

Noah rushed out of the room and disappeared.

Vincent was hesitant to say anything. He stuffed his hands in his pockets and raised his eyebrows, gesturing he was uncomfortable.

"I'm sure you have other things to do, like defend your palace," Bridgette said, now snapping at Vincent.

"I thought I could hang around and help with anything you need."

The strain on Bridgette's face subsided for a second but went right back up. "No need, we can take care of this."

"It's not any trouble. You look like you could use some help."

"We'll be fine; there really isn't anything else we need from you."

Vincent wasn't shocked by her comments. He had seen this before and knew it was her painful emotions speaking not the real person. This knowledge gave him sympathy for her and made him want to stay and help even more.

"Thank you again for trying, but we really will be fine. You know where the door is," Bridgette said and left the room.

He heard her stomping footsteps rush back upstairs and into the master bedroom. When the door slammed, he cringed. The pain, fear and uncertainty she must be experiencing had to be overwhelming, he thought. Knowing that insisting on helping would only backfire, he grabbed his things and left.

Outside the driver's door of the SUV, he stopped when he felt eyes on him. He turned and looked back towards the house; his gaze found the source. Noah was standing in a window on the second floor. He didn't wave or move, he just stood staring. Vincent knew whatever Bridgette was feeling, Noah felt tenfold. A child looks to their parents for strength and protection, and when that's not there, it throws them off and leaves them in a place that is dark. He was sure Noah must be there and Vincent had to find a way to help, but timing was everything, as was his approach.

With a smile on his face, Vincent raised his arm and waved at Noah, and just before he lowered his arm, he mouthed the words, 'I'll be back.'

Undisclosed Bunker Facility, Superstition Mountains, East of Apache Junction, Arizona

Michael had asked for the chance to go outside and get fresh air, and Anatoly had granted it. The warmth of the desert sun felt good on his face, and the smell of the dry air made it even better. He loved the desert but especially loved the Sonoran Desert above all he had ever visited. Its rugged terrain, reddish brown colors and unique fauna made it so beautiful to him.

Once outside he could see that their location was remote, and nothing around him looked familiar. His trip outside also gave him confirmation on his assumption that the facility was desolate. He counted three men guarding the entrance, but besides them he saw no one as Karina escorted him through the maze of hallways and stairwells to the exit. This gave him mixed feelings. If he wanted to escape, he wouldn't have to worry about fighting an army to leave, but if he needed them to protect him against Viktor, there weren't many of them to put up a defense.

He had spent most of the night thinking about the information Anatoly had disclosed to him. Again, he found it all odd but at the same time strangely familiar. It was this familiarity that he clung to. He eventually passed out from exhaustion but woke only to continue the frustrating process of remembering. As he tried to take a moment to enjoy himself, he quickly went back to trying to piece it all together. Unable to do so, he began to recite what he did know.

He distinctly remembered being in the military; he had a clear vision of his years as a Ranger. He knew he had been a CIA operative and even remembered his early years of training. Only when it came to recent memories did he have issues. He knew he had been on that ship, the very one that was the launching pad for the EMP. He knew some man named Viktor was trying to kill him; he had memories of that. He had distinct memories of Karina and felt they were more than colleagues. His mind then went to family, maybe there he'd be able to put it together, start from the last time he talked to or had seen his brother, Nicholas. He recalled that Nicholas and his family lived in the San Diego area, but he couldn't recall the last time he'd been there.

Frustrated that most of his memories were a blur or, worse, blank, void of anything, he stopped his pacing and sat on the ground and rested his back against the rough concrete wall. He placed his face in his hands and squeezed. Maybe he could forcibly press his memories out.

The sound of hard soles on tiny pieces of gravel snapped him out of his futile exercise. He looked up and saw Karina, which brought a smile to his face.

"How are you doing?" she asked.

"Nothing new, I was just sitting here, trying to force my brain to work."

"Anatoly and I were talking, and we think that we might have an idea."

"Oh yeah, please tell me it doesn't require drugs or

electrodes," he joked.

"Nothing painful, I can assure you of that," she said and offered her hand to assist him in getting up.

He took her small hand and lifted himself to his feet. "So what's this idea?"

"I think you'll like it. In fact, I'd be surprised if you didn't," she said with a smile then winked.

"Hmm, sounds intriguing."

She led him back down through the labyrinth of seemingly endless hallways until they came to a metal door. It was no different than any other door along the hallway. She produced a key from her pocket, inserted it into the lock and turned it.

He could hear the tumbler turn and click.

She opened the door and pushed it open. "Please, go inside."

He hesitated, not because he was afraid, but because he had grown a healthy skepticism of all things new.

Noticing his hesitation, she said, "No one is in there, I promise."

He looked into her eyes and saw the woman from his memories, and that woman never hurt him. He forced himself to trust the situation, so he stepped into the darkness.

She came in right behind him and closed the door, leaving the light from the hallway outside.

"Aren't there any lights in here?" he asked, stopping the second the door closed. A strong whiff of perfume hit his nose followed by the gentle touch of her hand on his neck. "Ahh, why don't we turn on some lights."

"Sshh," she cooed.

He recognized that tone in her voice and his fear began to turn to arousal.

Her hand worked its way from his neck to his hand. She took it and lifted his arm and placed his hand on her bare breast.

"How did you get undressed so quickly?" he asked with nervousness in his voice.

She then led him through the dark for several feet and stopped. She let go of his hand and stepped away.

"Where did you go?" he asked. He couldn't believe how dark the room was.

The distinct sound of a match striking then the orange glow startled him. He turned and saw her now naked form standing a few feet away. In her hands she held the flaming match and used it to light a small candle. When the candle's wick took the flame, she brought the match close to her lips and just before she blew it out, she looked at him.

The light from the match enhanced the seductiveness of her gaze for him.

Pouting her lips, she blew out the candle.

Michael's eyes took in all of her slender curves and asked, "Exactly whose idea was this, yours or Anatoly's?"

She stepped up to him and began to strip him of his clothes. She unbuttoned his pants, pushed them down and said, "Stop talking and make love to me like you used to."

Wellsville, Utah

Nicholas arrived on time for an impromptu meeting with Chad, the mayor, but found him busy when he arrived. Sitting in a chair outside his office, he heard loud talking and an occasional yell. Whatever the topic was inside, it was definitely heated.

The door opened and the man he recognized as Chuck Summers stood in the doorway, his face flush and his jaw clenched.

"Chuck, you square that boy away, you hear me! I don't want to hear anything else about him or what he thinks he knows," Chad barked.

Chuck leered at Chad and replied, "Mr. Mayor, remember who helped get you elected. Okay, this isn't my mess to begin with, it's yours, and sending your son out there to clean up loose ends isn't the way we should be dealing with this."

Chad looked past Chuck and saw Nicholas sitting in the hall. "Close the door, would you? We're not done."

Chuck looked at Nicholas and then shut the door.

Again they went back and forth until everything went silent. The door opened again and Chuck rushed out. His face was still flush and his hands were curled up into fists.

Nicholas watched him march out of the city offices, slamming the exterior door behind him.

"Mr. McNeil, come in, come in," Chad said.

Nicholas did as he said and stepped into the office, closing the door behind him. "I can come back another time."

"No, just some city business, politics. Anyways, thank you for coming on short notice. I wanted to see how your first night was," Chad said as he wheeled around his desk and stopped just in front of Nicholas.

"It was good, thank you. It's always nice to sleep in a bed," Nicholas replied, a bit disturbed that he only wanted to ask about his first night.

"Can I get you a drink?" Chad asked, making his way past Nicholas, who was standing at the front of his desk.

"I thought Mormons didn't drink." Nicholas snorted.

"Who said we were *all* Mormons?" Chad asked as he poured a couple fingers of whiskey into a glass.

"You're not?"

"I'll be honest with you, Nicholas, and I hope you'll be so with me."

"Honest?"

"Yes, honesty is the best policy," Chad said and spun around in his wheelchair while balancing the glass in his lap.

"Sure."

"Glad to hear it," Chad said and took a sip. "I'll be very sad when I run out of the good stuff," he continued as he admired the glass. "You sure I can't get you some?"

Nicholas felt tempted to have a glass but resisted. He wanted to stay clear and focused. "None for me."

"I guess you could call me a Jack Mormon."

"What's that?"

"It's had a couple meanings over the years, but now it mainly represents someone who was once devoted to the faith but is no longer. I was born and raised in this great little town, and the only time I left her was when I went to college at BYU. Upon graduation I came back and worked for my family's business. My grandfather started and operated a small gravel pit not far from here. My father inherited the business and made it into one of the largest operations in Utah. I then took over for him and turned it into one of the largest in the West. I would have passed it onto my children, but someone offered me a deal I couldn't refuse," Chad said and paused to take another sip. He again looked at his glass and continued, "They say everyone has a price; I'm an example of that. I sold my children's legacy, but I gave them a trust fund most would only dream of."

Nicholas could see the disappointment in his eyes.

"And you know what they did with it? They took the money and went somewhere else to live; no reason to stay here when there wasn't a company to help run. Nope, they took the cash and left, except my eldest, he stayed."

"I've always heard the eldest is the most loyal."

"What about you, any siblings?"

"Just an older brother," Nicholas replied. He was growing weary of the conversation and his side was aching.

"How come your brother is not with you?"

"Is there something you wanted? I don't like being away from my family. I don't mean to be abrupt, but if this was just about having a casual conversation, could we do it another time?" Nicholas declared.

Chad acted as if he hadn't heard Nicholas. He tipped his glass back and finished it. "Have you spoken to your group about staying?"

"Yes, and we want to wait until the other two get back

here before we make any final decision."

"I can understand wanting to wait. Hopefully, we'll find your friends soon; I've got my best trying to find them."

"And for that, I thank you."

"Would you care to join me, my son and some other townsfolk for a welcoming picnic tomorrow night in the park across the street? We have some steaks, fresh from a ranch I have just outside of town. I'd love to sit and just chat, more personal like," Chad offered.

Nicholas didn't care much for social time with people he didn't know, but he figured it was necessary to placate his hosts; after all, they had helped him and were looking for Bryn. "Sure, I assume that invite goes out to my wife and daughter?"

"Of course, in fact, bring the whole group. Brock will come and get you. Now if you'll excuse me, I have a meeting," Chad said as he wheeled past Nicholas and out of the office.

Nicholas watched him go and took a moment to look around the ornate office. On the wall behind is massive oak desk hung a large framed oil painting of Mormon pioneers heading into the Great Salt Lake area. On top of file drawers beneath it were framed photos of Chad with people. Nicholas leaned in to take a closer look, but he stopped when he heard someone enter the office.

"Can I help you?" said Sally, Chad's secretary.

"Oh no, sorry, was just leaving. I always like to look at family photos."

"It's so sad what happened to his family, so very sad."

Nicholas raised his eyebrows and asked, "What happened?"

Sally was about to tell him but stopped short, "That's a conversation for you and the mayor to have; it's not my place to discuss private matters."

"Quite right."

"I need to close up his office, do you mind?" Sally asked.

"Sure thing," Nicholas replied and swiftly left only to walk into a small group of people. By the looks of them, they were fellow travelers like him. He could tell by the weary and disheveled look on their faces.

They were being escorted down the hall towards the same conference room where he'd first met Chad yesterday.

Nicholas thought the highway must bring many prospects in for Chad and his town. He understood Chad's desire to have more people, and the offer to stay in a safe and seemingly robust town was tempting, but he still needed to make sure it was the right move. So far all appeared about right, even the odd meeting this morning wasn't too out of sorts. He chalked it up to Chad doing his own due diligence on Nicholas.

Tomorrow they'd have more time to talk and ask questions. Until then, he needed to make sure they were ready to bounce at a moment's notice.

Undisclosed Bunker Facility, Superstition Mountains, East of Apache Junction, Arizona

"Oh my God," Michael said, gleaming.

"Looks like you haven't forgotten how to do that," Karina purred and kissed his neck.

Michael looked at Karina, who was now cradling his torso, and asked, "Were we really close?"

She lifted her head and shot him a look of irritation. "You really can't remember?"

"Like I've said before, things are familiar, but the details aren't there. It's as if I remember you, but you aren't really my memory. Does that sound strange?"

"What did Viktor do to you?"

"Apparently a lot," Michael said and shifted in the bed. "I'm sorry."

"Don't be. We will get this working again," she said and placed her index finger on his lips. "I'm just glad we don't have to find a way to get this working." She then placed her other hand on his crotch.

He smiled but quickly shifted it to a frown. Her renewed sexual attention wasn't enough to stop him from being troubled. "I was thinking about my brother and was curious if you ever met him?"

"No."

"When we were together, did I ever talk about him?"

"Yes, but all I know is he lived in San Diego. Nothing more than that," Karina answered as she propped herself up.

"I know what you're doing here. You're hoping that if we reconnect, that it will somehow jog my memory."

"Yes, but don't think I don't want you, I do. We were engaged before all this happened."

"We were?"

"Yes, you gave me this," Karina said, holding up a ring that hung from a gold necklace.

He exhaled deeply and said, "I don't remember any of that."

She looked at the ring and cracked a smile, but her smile turned down. Tears welled in her eyes and she fell onto the pillow next to him.

"What I don't understand is why didn't I give you the coordinates before if we were working together?"

Karina didn't answer; she lay next to him, staring at the ring.

He looked over and saw she was crying. "Why are you crying?"

"You don't remember anything; especially the night you told me you loved me. You don't remember the day you proposed to me. It just makes me sad."

Michael rolled onto his side and took her hand. "I will do everything I can to remember those details, but what I can tell you for sure is I feel close to you. I feel in my heart you were someone I cared about deeply. Just give me a bit more time."

"We don't have time, Michael."

"Was there anything you can tell me about the last time we were together?"

She thought and replied, "The last time I saw you was

six months ago. You left to go undercover to stop Viktor's plan."

"I didn't say anything about the coordinates?"

"You didn't know them then."

"Then why do you think I know them now?"

"Because your last communication to me was that the coordinates were in your possession but that you were sending them somewhere safe so Viktor wouldn't get them."

Michael chewed on his lip as he pondered where that might be. He knew of no place safe, at least that he could remember. He had no parents, but he did have family and that was Nicholas. Suddenly, like a light bulb going off, he spat out, "I gave them to Nicholas. I gave the coordinates to my brother!"

CHAPTER FOUR

"In any moment of decision, the best thing you can do is the right thing, the next best thing is the wrong thing, and the worst thing you can do is nothing." – Theodore Roosevelt

Wellsville, Utah

Chad had honored his word a second time and provided not only beautiful wildflowers but also a casket, burial plot and stone for Proctor's funeral.

All of this went way beyond what Nicholas expected and even impressed him. However, Nicholas was having a difficult time emotionally dealing with the loss of his old friend. And the thought of going to a funeral for someone he cared for was not something he wanted to experience. If it was his doing, he wouldn't have had one for Proctor, not because he didn't care or respect him but for the fact that funerals had a way of making it final. Nicholas kept this little secret hidden from most, he disliked with a passion saying goodbye, and for him a funeral was the ultimate goodbye. From an early age, Nicholas would not come out to kiss his grandparents goodbye when they were gathering their belongings to leave, he'd hide so no one could find him.

Becky had tried multiple times to dig and find the why, but Nicholas knew and didn't care to share. The loss of his parents at a young age and the experience at their funeral forever changed him. To him as a boy, he remembered seeing them one day, then the next he was told they were dead. Nicholas hadn't wanted to believe it, for days after he'd tell himself that they were still gone on a trip and would be back one day, but when he saw their cold corpses lying in the casket, he knew he couldn't lie anymore. The cold hard truth was right there in front of him, and no matter how much he tried to blot out the vision of them at the funeral home, he couldn't. They were dead and *never* coming back. And now he knew today that Proctor was also dead and would never be there by his side; he'd never hear his laugh or listen to him explain his theories over beers, especially the signature slur he'd get after one too many. Looking at his body in the casket told him that Proctor was gone forever.

Becky found herself not only consoling Katherine and Evelyn but giving extra attention to Nicholas.

"What time is the picnic?" she asked, referring to Chad's town picnic he was organizing for the new arrivals. The two were walking slowly back to the Suburban. The rest of the group was following closely behind.

"I have zero desire to go to that. Do you think if we skipped it, they'd notice?" Nicholas answered, his tone obviously somber.

"Believe me, it's the last thing I want to do, but we should."

Nicholas didn't hear Becky, his thoughts were on Katherine. He stopped and turned back towards the cemetery. "I think I should stay with her."

"I asked her if I could stay and she flatly said no."

"I feel bad just leaving her here," Nicholas moaned.

"She said for us to go and that's what we should do. We can't go around imposing ourselves on others."

The roar of cars traveling at high speed broke the quiet.

Nicholas turned to see what was going on. In the distance he could see two older trucks speeding at breakneck speed down the main road, their tires squealing when they were making turns.

"That doesn't look good," Colin said.

"No, it doesn't," Nicholas replied.

The crack and whine of a handheld radio suddenly sounded from their vehicle.

Colin and Nicholas both sprinted towards it. Their curiosity piqued as to what emergency was occurring.

"Get the ER up and ready. We're bringing two in!" a voice said from the handset.

"This is the hospital. We copy, two coming in. What's their conditions?" the hospital replied.

"Multiple gunshot wounds to the abdomen, bleeding badly. We'll need extra blood for sure!"

"Okay, do we need to contact next of kin?" the hospital replied.

"Yes, contact the mayor on the secondary channel and contact..." the radio crackled and broke up.

"You broke up; you said, contact the mayor and who?" the hospital asked.

"Contact Nicholas McNeil. We found his friends."

Undisclosed Bunker Facility, Superstition Mountains, East of Apache Junction, Arizona

"Anatoly, you keep repeating over and over again that you don't think it's a good idea for me to go with you. You doing so doesn't make me change my mind any more than it did the first time. I'm going, and Karina is on my side," Michael snapped at Anatoly.

Michael's revelation last night was a critical clue to them finding the coordinates to the location of the Spear, but Anatoly felt it best for Michael to stay. The bunker provided security, and if he was captured by Viktor, all could be lost.

"Mikhail, you need to stay. We cannot risk losing you again," Anatoly said.

"It doesn't make sense. The trip to my brother's will likely help my memory," Michael said defensively.

"I agree with Michael," Karina added.

"And how is it that you don't have any support? You have this enormous bunker but no people or assets?" Michael challenged.

"Most of our people are either dead or out fighting against Viktor," Anatoly explained.

"That's true," Karina confirmed.

"Anatoly, I'm going, so let's get going. We don't have much time," Michael said.

Anatoly stared at Michael; he had the power to stop him but decided to give in.

"I'll have clothes and equipment sent to your room; get

yourself ready. We leave in two hours," Anatoly said and marched off, leaving Karina and Michael standing in the conference room.

"I hope my brother is there. Seeing him will help me, I know it," Michael said, his face clearly showing his happiness.

Karina leaned in gave him a kiss on the lips. "I'm happy for you; I hope your brother is there too."

Michael returned the kiss. He then pulled back and asked, "What did Anatoly mean when he said I was more than a CIA agent?"

"I was curious when you were going to ask about that," Karina said.

"Well?"

"For someone who lost their memory, everything we've told you sounds strange, so this will just add to it. You are more than anything you've ever been in your life. It's in your blood to serve and protect," she said and chuckled.

"What's so funny?"

"Just that I'm having this conversation with you once again. I told you about your legacy a couple years ago when we met in Budapest. I remember when I first saw your handsome and beautiful face. Now look at you, it's covered in bruises and cuts, and that wonderful strong nose of yours is broken," she said and again laughed.

"Is my face that messed up now it's funny?"

"When you and I became intimate, I told you that I'd stop seeing you if you lost your teeth."

Michael touched his teeth as if he might have forgotten

whether he'd lost any recently.

"They're all there, you're lucky; otherwise yesterday would not have happened," she teased.

The more she talked, the more his attraction grew for her. He could see why they were engaged, he was totally enthralled with her.

"Sorry, I digressed. Your legacy has always been to protect the Spear and other powerful relics. Your father did it, and you were then given the responsibility for your family."

"What about Nicholas?"

"Only the oldest child is given the task; he knows nothing about this."

"How do you know this Spear is real or that it has power?" Michael asked, genuinely curious but also highly skeptical.

"Faith."

"Like religious?"

"More like spiritual."

"But you don't know for sure this Spear actually holds the power you say it does?"

"All we know is what we've been told. We are the Knights of the Sacred Antiquities, but we just call ourselves the Knights."

Michael cracked a broad smile.

She punched him and asked, "Now what do you think is so funny?"

"Knights of the Sacred Antiquities, really? It sounds so Indiana Jones or something out of a fantasy novel."

"This is exactly how you acted before."

"You have to admit, it all sounds so…"

"So what?"

"Silly."

Her jovial and playful expression suddenly changed. "There's nothing silly about it. It's not a game. We've lost many of our Knights protecting the ancient relics and a good number trying to protect you. There's nothing silly about what Viktor has done and will do."

Michael couldn't help but feel that this was all so odd and that Viktor had to be a mad and delusional man. Regardless of whether the Spear was truly powerful, Viktor thought it was and would stop at nothing to get it.

"How exactly did Viktor get so powerful that he came into possession of a super-EMP?" Michael asked, shifting his questions to something else.

"Viktor was once the Russian defense minister, so it was rather easy for him."

"But why cause so much chaos and destruction? Why not just get the spear first, do it covertly?"

"His plan has always been to take over the world with or without the spear. He thought it easier to complete his task of finding it if the world was turned on itself."

Michael's head was again swimming with endless questions. He looked up at the clock and saw they had burned too much time. "Let's continue this conversation later; we have a long drive."

"Drive? We're not driving anywhere. We'll be at your brother's house by early afternoon."

"We're flying?"

"As the old Michael use to say, that's how we roll."

Vista, CA

Vincent had risen with the sun and went to work preparing an elaborate breakfast for Bridgette and Noah. He knew she might turn him away, but at least he'd make an attempt at providing comfort for them in their time of need.

After finding a basket in the garage and loading up everything, he made his way towards their house. The first thing he saw that made him feel uneasy about his little sojourn there was that their gate was unlocked and slighty ajar. He knew for a fact that when he left, he closed and secured it. Immediately his training kicked in as he surveyed the area, looking for anything out of place, but all seemed fine.

He pulled down the driveway, and off to the side of the house, he saw a pile of freshly dug dirt and a shovel. He knew it was Ron's grave even without seeing the homemade cross lying on the ground. He stopped just out front and took a few seconds to look around, again seeing if something seemed out of place, but not finding one thing.

He opened the door and as usual climbed out carefully, ensuring his foot didn't bump anything. The day could not come soon enough for his foot to heal, but a broken bone took time, and until then he'd have to keep adjusting and adapting. Vincent slung his rifle and began his slow advance towards the house on his crutches. The temptation to holler out for them came, but he didn't want to draw attention to his approach just in case. He reached the front door and tried the handle only to find it locked.

The blinds in a window to the right of him were up; he leaned over and looked in. He saw the couch he had slept on looked exactly like he had left it, the pillow and blanket still there.

"Noah?" Bridgette called from inside.

By the sound of her voice, she didn't seem in trouble, so Vincent decided to knock.

Bridgette's head appeared in the right window. She glared at him and went to the door, unlocked and opened it.

"Hi," Vincent said.

"What do you want?"

"I was thinking you'd be hungry, so I made a big breakfast and brought it over."

She looked at him and said, "I told you, we're fine."

"Listen, it's just a neighborly gesture. I'm not asking to eat with you."

Bridgette ignored what he said and began to close the door.

He stuck his foot in the door jamb, stopping it from closing, "Please, at least give the fresh food to Noah."

"Get your foot out of the way," she barked.

"So that's it, this is how you treat the man who gives you medicine and then tried to help by performing surgery on your dying husband. Once I'm not needed, you act like this. Let me tell you, if you think your conduct will keep you alive, it won't."

"I don't care to live anymore, so I don't give two shits."

"And Noah, what about him? Are you also making up his mind for him?" Vincent shot back.

"He's my son."

"He's a scared young boy, and if you gave a damn, you'd think twice about what you're doing."

"Just leave me alone!" she yelled.

Vincent opened his mouth to speak but stopped when Noah's yells echoed from the far end of the driveway.

"Help, Mom, help!" Noah screamed.

Vincent pivoted and saw the boy racing over the rise in the driveway at breakneck speed. Not wasting time to see what or who he was running from, Vincent pulled his pistol, handed it to Bridgette and ordered, "Take this, just in case you can't get to your other in time."

She too didn't hesitate; she took it and held it firmly in her grip.

Vincent still couldn't see why Noah was running, but whatever it was had the boy terrified. He hobbled away from the front door and towards his SUV.

Finally the reason Noah was running appeared over the hill. A pair of old motorcycles, one with a sidecar, sped down the driveway and were closing on Noah.

Vincent dropped his crutches, raised his rifle and leaned against the SUV. He took aim through his optics on the motorcycle in front while simultaneously flicking off the selector switch. His right index finger began to apply a steady pressure to the trigger until it discharged. The round hit the person driving squarely, causing them to slump forward, which turned the handlebars and the motorcycle into the path of the other. Both motorcycles collided in spectacular fashion. The person driving the second bike flew over their handlebars and landed helmet first into the gravel road. The person tucked in the sidecar found themselves bouncing around as it tumbled end over end, finally resting upside down.

Noah didn't stop running; he made it to Vincent and kept moving until he reached Bridgette.

Vincent couldn't help but be impressed with what one shot had accomplished. He stepped away from the SUV and picked up a single crutch. "Go inside, lock the door, and wait for me to come back!" he ordered Bridgette and Noah. He slowly hobbled towards the wreckage, using one crutch to minimize using his broken foot while keeping the rifle ready in his shoulder. It wasn't the easiest thing to do, but he made it work. The first thing he came upon was the person who had flown over their handlebars.

They were alive but appeared badly injured as they slowly crawled, clenching the gravel with their gloved hands.

Vincent leveled his rifle at them and asked, "Any more with you?"

The person rolled onto their side and pulled off their helmet.

Vincent wasn't expecting it to be a woman.

"Help," she begged. Blood streamed from a deep cut on her forehead.

"Help?"

A cry from the sidecar drew Vincent's attention. He looked over and saw the person squirming underneath the weight of the sidecar.

"My son, help him," the woman pleaded.

Vincent was in shock. He'd fully expected to find three

deranged men, but so far he'd come across a middle-aged woman and what sounded like a teenage boy.

The woman was clad from head to toe in tight black leather. She reached up with a quivering hand and began to unzip her jacket.

Vincent kicked her hand away and nearly lost his balance. "Don't do anything stupid. Are there others with you?"

She nodded that there was.

"Where are they?"

"Help my son," was her only reply.

The cries for help grew louder from underneath the sidecar.

Vincent firmed up his stance and asked, "Are you armed?"

"No," she said as the blood covered her face. She swallowed hard and again begged, "Please go help my son."

"Open your jacket; I need to make sure you're not armed."

The woman reached up and began to slowly unzip the jacket.

The cries from the sidecar grew even more intense.

"How far are your friends?" Vincent asked.

"I'll tell you, but you have to help my son," she countered.

The woman's expression suddenly changed as she looked past Vincent.

He turned and saw Bridgette coming; she was marching towards them, her feet stomping hard. She held the pistol tightly in her right hand.

"I said to stay in the house," Vincent said.

The woman unzipped quickly and went for a pistol tucked in her waistband.

Bridgette leveled the pistol and pulled the trigger twice. Both bullets hit the woman in the chest.

Vincent jumped back and, like a spectator, watched Bridgette kill the woman then move towards the sidecar.

"What are you doing?" Vincent asked.

"Doing what you're obviously incapable of," she answered then stopped at the sidecar and pulled the trigger several more times, killing the boy.

"That was a boy!" Vincent cried.

She turned back around and began to march back. As she passed him, she said, "That wasn't a boy, that was a monster."

"How do you know?"

She stopped and said, "Ask Noah what happened; then tell me what I did was wrong."

Wellsville, Utah

For the second time in days, Nicholas was confronted with another death from his group and the task of telling their loved one; this time it was Abigail.

The small clinic that served as the Wellsville hospital buzzed with activity. The news that some of their own had been hurt traveled fast. Townspeople had heeded the call for blood and were flooding in to donate.

Nicholas had seen Chad come in, but didn't get a chance to speak to him. The mayor was rushed through the crowd and disappeared down the hall.

The information Nicholas had gotten from the Wellsville security team that had been on site was sketchy, but it appeared that Bryn and Rob opened fire on Brock and a small team after being confronted near the old Dodge. From the few details and how Nicholas was being treated, it sounded as if Bryn and Rob were to blame and were the first to fire.

Bryn had been hit but had managed to flee in the car only to crash it further down the road.

Brock's team, which included Logan, had taken her to the hospital for treatment of her wounds, but she was under arrest. No one from their group, including Nicholas, would be allowed to see her after her surgery to remove two bullets that had hit her arm and shoulder. Bryn hadn't yet fully recovered from her last gunshot wound, but now she was wounded again and this time in trouble.

"I demand to see her the second she comes out of surgery," Nicholas said.

"Not going to happen, not until we question her," Logan said.

"Question her? This is dumb. If she fired, it was because she doesn't trust anyone. It's an honest mistake."

"Regardless, we have laws here, and we need to do an investigation," Logan said.

"So what? She shot first; you guys killed one of ours!" Nicholas barked.

"Only after they began shooting at us."

Nicholas' veins were bursting from his head as his temper grew.

Abigail ran down the hall, crying, "Where is he?"

Nicholas stopped her and said, "I told you to stay at the house."

"Dad, where is he?"

Nicholas didn't want to be the bearer of bad news, but she needed to know. "Honey, Rob was killed."

Abigail began to wail and clenched onto Nicholas. "It's all my fault. I should've never voted to go. I caused this. I'm so stupid."

"It's not your fault, honey, it's mine," Nicholas said in an attempt to console her.

She tucked her head in Nicholas' chest and continued to cry.

Nicholas looked at Logan, who gave a slight nod, indicating he understood this was a personal time. However, Nicholas wasn't done with the conversation. "I need to see Bryn the second she's out."

Logan shook his head and replied, "Not going to happen."

"I'll get permission from the mayor; he'll okay it."

"I doubt that."

"She only fired from fear, nothing more."

"It was more, she severely wounded Brock."

This was the first Nicholas had heard of Brock's condition. "But on the radio I heard only two reported shot."

"Two reported wounded; Rob died at the scene."

"How's he doing?" Nicholas asked with genuine

concern.

"She shot him up good; he took several shots to the chest."

"I'm sure the mayor will understand it was all an unfortunate accident," Nicholas lamented, his fiery tone gone.

Logan shrugged his shoulders and replied, "Not sure, this is a bit personal for the mayor. Brock is his son."

Carlsbad, CA

The whoosh of the helicopter brought dozens of people out from their homes to investigate what was happening. The residents of Rancho Del Sur hadn't seen a helicopter since everything stopped working weeks before. So when the CH-47 Chinook spun around and made a soft landing in the large cul-de-sac at the end of Nicholas' old street, they had hoped to see government officials coming to save them. However, when the rear ramp lowered, their hopes were crushed. A team of six men wearing black and heavily armed rushed out and secured the perimeter. Just by their appearance, the people of Rancho Del Sur knew this wasn't help.

Fathers and mothers told their children to go hide, and those who had weapons brought them to the ready for a fight if necessary.

Following closely behind the security team were Anatoly, Karina and Michael.

Michael pointed up the street and said, "His house is five doors down on the right."

"Are you sure?" Anatoly asked.

"Yeah, my brother has lived here for years and this, for some reason, I remember," Michael said. He turned and continued, "In fact, I'll prove my memory for this place is solid. Over there is a trailhead that leads you down towards that road."

Anatoly looked and saw a sign that read 'TRAIL'. He looked back at Michael and nodded. He then turned to the security and ordered, "You, you and you, come with us."

Michael, not sure of what to expect, had requested a rifle and pistol and had been given both. Not wishing to stay in the street any longer than they needed to, Michael walked briskly up the hill towards Nicholas' house. He scanned the area and took notice of how the neighborhood's manicured look had deteriorated. The green grasses that lined the street were overgrown and turning brown. Trash, debris, abandoned cars and other types of litter lay on the street and sidewalks. The hoods of all the cars in view were up as their owners made a desperate but futile attempt to get them running again.

Michael saw dozens of eyes on him but felt dozens more. He, like Anatoly, agreed that this mission had to be quick. The helicopter was a tempting morsel, and the longer they sat, the greater the chance was to lose it. One thing in this world worse than someone in need was someone desperate with nothing to lose.

A woman holding a swaddled newborn baby came running towards them. "Are you here to help? Please help us."

A man, most likely her husband, chased after her. "Lisa, come back here. I don't think those people are here to help!"

The man on point security raised his rifle and aimed.

Michael saw this and rushed him. "Don't you dare shoot that woman!" he said, batting down the barrel.

"Lisa, come back!" the woman's husband pleaded.

Lisa stopped and froze when she saw what happened between Michael and the security man. She knew instantly that they could be more of a threat than helpful.

The point security man glared at Michael and snapped, "Don't fucking do that again."

"Don't shoot women holding babies."

"Everyone shut up and keep moving," Anatoly barked.

Michael returned the hard stare from the security man and moved on.

Karina ran up alongside Michael and said, "His name is Francis. I don't like him either."

"With a name like Francis, I can see why he has anger problems," Michael joked and kept walking. When he crested the hill and stood at the end of the debris-ridden driveway, his heart dropped. The garage door was open and Nicholas' Mercedes and BMW were sitting there with the doors and trunk left open. More debris and trash extended from the garage into the driveway. To the right, the front door was open and the same trail of debris came from it. There was no doubt in his mind that the house held no occupants. He just prayed he wouldn't find their bodies inside.

Karina stepped beside him and said, "I'm so sorry, my sweet." She looked at the condition of the house and surmised the same thing as Michael.

Anatoly brushed by with two security men and proceeded down the driveway and into the house through the garage.

Michael and Karina followed Anatoly and found the same inside.

"Nicholas, it's Michael!" Michael cried out, his voice echoing off the still walls.

The house had been ransacked, the kitchen taking the brunt of the invasion.

A member of the security team came into the kitchen and said, "The house is clear. No one is here."

"Any bodies?" Michael asked.

"No, sir."

"Well, they're gone, not surprising," Michael said as he paced around, looking at the terrible condition of the house.

"The next question is, where are they?" Karina said.

"They could be anywhere," Anatoly exclaimed.

"He wouldn't have taken his family just anywhere; Nic isn't like that," Michael said.

"Your memory seems fine when it pertains to your brother." Anatoly smirked.

"My memory is fine now, but anything over the past year seems foggy, so it makes sense that I know who my brother is and what he might have done," Michael countered.

"Then you should know where they went," Anatoly

said.

Francis walked in with an armful of framed photos and set them on the counter. "Maybe one of these might help tell us where they might have gone."

"Pictures of family?" Anatoly asked.

Michael looked at the stack of frames and the sight gave him a name. "Uncle Jim, I would bet my last dollar they went to Becky's uncle Jim's house in Montana. It makes sense for Nicholas to take his family somewhere they'd have a chance to survive."

"But how would he get there?" Karina asked.

"That's a good question."

"Hence why they could be anywhere in between here and Montana," Anatoly said, again inserting his negativity.

"Or they could already be in Montana. We should go," Michael asserted.

"Michael, I need you to think hard before we go. We're here; we need to take time to search the house. You need to think very, very hard about why you think Nicholas has the coordinates and just how you gave them to him," Karina said.

"She's right," Anatoly added.

Michael looked at them both. He wanted to argue for leaving now, but her point was valid. "Okay, let me start in his office," Michael said and left the kitchen on his way to Nicholas' office.

Vista, CA

"You two can sleep in the upstairs master bedroom," Vincent suggested.

After the altercation, Bridgette asked and Vincent immediately agreed to her and Noah coming to stay at the compound. Several times she referred to it as his place or house, but when he mentioned the property, he called it the compound. Even though Roger had given him the house and land, he just didn't feel right calling it his.

"Goodnight, mister," Noah said.

Just then Vincent remembered he had never formally introduced himself. "Just call me Gunner."

"That's a cool name," Noah replied.

"I think so too. How about dinner?"

"Upstairs, you," Bridgette ordered. She turned and quickly said, "Good night." She rushed up the stairs behind Noah and disappeared.

"I guess that means no on the dinner," Vincent joked. He could feel his foot throbbing. Without a doubt the incident today didn't help. With no one to entertain, he went about his nightly ritual of securing the house before making dinner.

The sun had set, leaving only darkness. Vincent lit candles throughout the house and in the kitchen ran a few LED lanterns to help illuminate while he prepared dinner.

"Smells good," Bridgette said from the doorway of the kitchen.

Vincent's attention was on stirring the refried beans he

had cooking in a saucepan. "I didn't hear you. I thought you were down for the night."

"I thought so too, but the aroma of those beans got to me."

"You like ole Mexican food?" Vincent joked.

"I live in Southern California, of course I do," she said and walked further into the kitchen. She took a seat on a bar stool next to the kitchen island.

"It's a nice house you have here. I looked around and saw some kids' rooms."

Vincent scooped out some beans and put them on a plastic plate and tossed on two warmed corn tortillas. He spun around and placed it in front of her. "What's the equivalent of bon appétit in Spanish?" he asked, not wanting to get into the house or why he was there.

She laughed and replied, "Not sure, but I'm so hungry."

Vincent scooped a plate for himself and set it across from her. He was happy to see her approachable and wanted to take advantage, so he grabbed a bottle of wine and brought it back. "Some vino?"

"Sure," she answered and dipped her tortilla in the beans.

Vincent found two glasses, pulled the cork and poured the wine. He set the bottle down and picked up his glass to toast. Ever since a young age he had seen his parents toast and recognize someone or something over a drink. So in honor of that tradition, he offered his glass but didn't know what to say.

She looked oddly at him but picked up her glass too.

She saw him hesitate, so as to not have him hanging, she said, "To you, thank you."

"Oh, not necessary."

"I have to apologize for my conduct earlier. To say I'm going through a lot doesn't seem to say enough."

Their glasses were still in the air; neither had taken a drink.

"I was going to toast to having a drink. It's been a while since I had someone to toast with," he joked and took a large drink.

She did the same and said, "That's pretty good."

He looked at the bottle and said, "It's Silver Oak Cabernet from Napa Valley, is that good?"

"Yes, it is, nice choice. You have good taste."

"Hmm, I'm not much of a wine person. If it was Boone's Farm, I'd be happy. Anything to take the edge off."

They exchanged small talk over the meal while pouring glass after glass of wine until they had finished the bottle. He went, got another and opened it.

After pouring another glass full, he said, "I thought about those bikers afterwards, and I have to admit I was too slow in dealing with them."

"I thought about it too. I want to make it known that I'm not some cold-blooded killer. When Noah told me what they did to him, I became enraged."

"What happened? Where did he go?"

"He snuck out to go get the damn cat he'd seen at the Taylor house. He saw that old tabby when we were there weeks ago; he felt bad for the old fleabag and wanted to bring it home. Without going into too much detail, they were scavengers and found him there. That kid who was pinned under the side car tried to sexually assault him, but Noah fought back and ran. God knows how that little guy was able to escape, but he did. He took a shortcut across a field, but they saw him from the road and followed him to our place. I have no doubt in my mind that if they had caught him, he'd be dead."

"I'm sorry that happened to him."

"I tell him over and over again to stop taking off. This time I think he learned his lesson."

"I'm not normally that guy that doesn't take care of business," Vincent said but was interrupted.

"No shit, I saw you race over, foot broken, and with one shot take them both down. No need to explain anything, trust me," she declared, wanting to defend him.

"Yeah, but I acted too slowly. I guess I was never expecting to see women and children acting like that. However, I should have known, I was held up the other day by a woman," he then added with a laugh.

"You see, I was just trying to train you."

"Cheers to that," he said and held his glass high.

She could feel the alcohol and welcomed it.

As he poured another glass, he said, "I like wine, but I love beer. Too bad they didn't have any."

She raised an eyebrow and asked him, "Whose house is this?"

Vincent gulped hard, thought about his answer, then wondered why he wouldn't be honest. What did he have to prove? he thought. "This isn't my house, although technically it is now since they gifted it to me before they left."

"Who would gift you a house like this?" she asked, a tone of doubt in her voice.

"They did, but how can you live so close to someone and not know your neighbors?"

"Don't divert; whose house is this?"

"Roger Puller and his family."

"So this is the famous Puller compound?" she asked, taking another drink.

"So you know them?"

"Know of them, they kept to themselves, very private people. Some say he was strange, very eccentric; you know, the crazy-billionaire type?"

"Actually, I don't. I'm just a Marine from Idaho."

"A Marine like from Camp Pendleton?"

"Yeah."

"Why aren't you there?"

"I'll tell you the short version. My helicopter crashed not far from here. Roger and his family saved me; they brought me here and patched me up. After several days they took off and left me the keys to the place."

"You still didn't explain why you're still here and not back on base."

"That's the million-dollar question, isn't it?" he asked then took a large drink. "My parents are in Idaho and they're getting up in age. If I went back, I'd probably never get a chance to check on them. I plan on going back one day, but not just yet. My plan is to head north very soon."

She finished her glass and pushed it towards him for a

refill. "I hope you know I wasn't serious about not wanting to live. I'm just emotional and that came out. My parents are older too and live in Oklahoma. Before Ron got hurt, our plan was to go there, but well, you know what happened. I'm looking at finding a way there, just not sure how that will happen without a car."

Knowing that she'd probably never make it to Oklahoma tugged at Vincent's heartstrings. They were two people with similar objectives, but only one had the means to accomplish it. He felt bad for her, but could he really give up on his parents to help a widow and her child?

She tipped the glass back again and emptied it with one large drink. A dribble of wine ran down her chin, making her laugh. "I think I might have had too much."

"One more for the night," Vincent insisted as he went to refill her glass.

"Nope, that's enough for little old me. I'm not much of a drinker and that was past my limit. Thank you for everything, Gunner, much appreciated." She stood and upon her first step staggered a bit. Catching herself, she chuckled, "See, a bit too much."

"Have a good night, Bridgette."

She stumbled out of the kitchen and up the stairs.

He was going to call it a night but looked at the half-full bottle and said, "Why not?" He filled his glass and walked into the living room. Finding the large leather cushion chair, he took a seat. The yellow glow from the candles cast flickering shadows across the room. He started to question his plan for Idaho. He knew what his father would tell him to do. In fact, his father would be disappointed in him as a man if he left her and Noah. Thoughts once again came up about the crash and why he survived it. It was a nagging question for him. Why did he live while the others died? He had heard of survivor's guilt and knew it was a symptom of PTSD but would never consider what he had as PTSD; that was for everyone else.

His father had been a large part of his life, and one lesson he had drilled into his head was that everything that happens in life has a meaning and not to find a negative meaning but a positive one. He had taken that lesson throughout his life and had been applying it to the crash. There was a reason he survived that crash and it probably wasn't to go home and check on his parents, it was to be helpful to those in need. He then thought of Bridgette and Noah and saw that fate had placed in front of him two people who needed help, so if that was fate's wish, he'd fulfill it.

CHAPTER FIVE

"There is no education like adversity." – Benjamin Disraeli

Wellsville, Utah

When Nicholas and the others received word that Bryn would survive her wounds, they rejoiced; however, that joy was quickly dashed when the word that followed told of Brock's death. Needless to say, it made for a difficult and tenuous night.

Nicholas didn't know what Brock's death would mean to Bryn or his group, but he was sure it wasn't good. He tried to reassure himself that Rob's and Brock's deaths equaled out, but deep down he knew that wouldn't be the case.

Almost in an instant the town's hospitality had ceased. The picnic that had been scheduled was canceled, and the evening was spent listening to howls and protest outside their house. Nicholas ordered they double up on watch for the night just to make sure no one tried anything stupid.

The new day did not bring new opportunities; in fact, it had proven to be tough for the group. When Nicholas and Sophie went to the hospital to visit Bryn, the security posted there refused them access. When he tried to go see

Chad at the city offices, he too refused to meet with him and had his security escort him away. The trouble for Bryn went directly to Chad's opening speech to Nicholas. In that speech, Chad mentioned the town's survival rested upon the rule of law, and it was obvious to Nicholas that rule of law was in full swing.

Nicholas couldn't just sit and wait. He had to find out what they should be expecting, plus he needed to get Rob's body, which no one seemed to know about.

Nicholas and Sophie returned to the city offices, and this time were not taking no for an answer. They walked in and decided to camp out until he returned.

"Mr. McNeil, the mayor does not wish to see you right now. As you can imagine, he's mourning his son," Sally informed.

"Tell Chad that I offer my condolences, but what is going on with my people is highly inappropriate," Nicholas countered.

"Mr. McNeil, he is not available, but maybe I can have you meet with someone from the council," Sally said, offering a solution.

Nicholas thought about the alternative and decided to take it; he figured that at least he'd be talking with someone that might be able to influence the circumstances for Bryn.

Sally walked them down to the conference room and told them to wait.

Seconds later a man walked in that Nicholas remembered meeting the other day.

"Tom Fielding, how can I help you?" he asked. Tom was middle-aged with premature graying hair and sported a small belly that jutted out. He stood just shy of six foot and at one time was the local star high school football player.

"Thanks for meeting with us," Nicholas said, standing and offering his hand. Nicholas was determined to play whatever political or congenial thing he had to in order to save Bryn.

"Not a problem, but you can imagine we have a lot we're dealing with, but I'm not sure how I can help."

"I'm Nicholas McNeil…"

"I know who you are, I remember you from the other day, but I don't know who this is," Tom said while looking at Sophie.

"Sophie, I'm Bryn's sister."

"Yes, your sister, Bryn. She's in a bit of trouble," Tom blurted out.

"That's why I want to meet with Chad and sort this out. Bryn is a good person, and this entire thing is being blown out of proportion," Nicholas declared.

Tom scrunched his face and asked, "You do know who Brock was?"

"Yes, I'm aware, but the thing was a mistake. She was only acting to defend herself from someone she didn't know. The world out there is not like it is in here."

Tom leaned on the table and placed both his elbows down. He exhaled heavily and said, "I don't know what I can do for you. The wheels of justice are moving forward. We are only able to function as a town if we have rules and laws."

Nicholas had to stop himself from jumping on Tom's comment about rules and laws. If he ever took the time to step out from the protective bubble they were living in, they'd see that while they have a set of laws, there's another when you're struggling to survive.

"I'm sorry, did Sally offer you guys something to drink?" Tom asked as he pivoted and showed the typical Wellsville hospitality.

"No, we don't want something to drink, we want to see our friend, and we want Rob's body released to us so we may bury him," Nicholas snapped.

Tom smiled and said, "No need to get upset, and I would highly suggest not barking at someone who might be able to help you."

"So you can help us?" Sophie asked enthusiastically.

"I can't make any guarantees, but Bryn will need legal representation, and there I can be of assistance," Tom said, showing his large white teeth as he smiled.

"Legal representation for what?"

"We run a tight ship around here, and the process has to go through its course."

Nicholas had heard enough. "This is complete bullshit. I want to see her and talk with her, now!"

"Now, now, please calm down. You getting upset won't make that any easier. Once they have talked with her."

"Oh, you mean interrogate!" Nicholas barked, interrupting Tom.

"Mr. McNeil, we don't interrogate people here. We just need to ask her a few questions."

Nicholas turned to Sophie and said, "This is unbelievable, this is truly unfucking believable." He then looked back at Tom and asked, "Doesn't she get to speak with an attorney or something, a phone call? Wait, hold on, I'm acting like this is some legitimate process. This is total bullshit. Bryn did nothing wrong; she defended herself, nothing more."

"I'm sorry you're so upset, but this is our system."

"Well, your system sucks."

"You wouldn't be sitting here if Brock, the man your friend murdered, hadn't saved you."

"Hold on, hold on, what did you just say?" Nicholas asked, his temper almost reaching a boiling-over point.

"Brock saved you."

"No, the other thing."

"I don't know what you mean," Tom said.

"You said murder."

"Yes, murder. Mr. McNeil, your friend will be charged with the murder of the mayor's son, Brock, later today. A swift trial will commence after that."

"And what if she's found guilty?" Sophie asked, her breathing rapid.

"Why, she'll be given a sentence, and that is…" Tom paused, knowing the next thing he said would not go over well. "Death."

Vista, CA

Vincent woke at first light to hear Noah playing in Zach's old room. Not wanting to disturb him, he peeked in and smiled. It was good seeing him be a kid.

A tinge of pain came from his head. It could only be one thing, a hangover. Wine wasn't his favorite alcoholic beverage, but when there's only so much to choose from, you take what you can get. He didn't mind the taste of it; it was the headaches he'd almost certainly get.

Down in the kitchen, he downed two tall glasses of water and hobbled around the house, checking the doors and looking outside.

Upon completing his tour of the house, he found Bridgette in the kitchen.

"Good morning," Vincent said, smiling. He had enjoyed his evening with her and felt like he had come to know her a bit better. He was also excited to talk about his plan to help her and Noah.

She didn't say anything, but stood staring out the window.

He hopped to the kitchen island and took a seat on a stool. "I'm feeling that wine this morning."

She still didn't say anything and didn't even turn to face him.

Concerned, he asked, "Do you have a raging headache like me? I hope not."

Finally speaking, she gave him a clue of where her mind was. "What has the world become?"

"The world has gone to shit," he replied.

"I was never one of those people who believed this could happen. I just never imagined that something this huge could happen. How did we allow this to happen? How?"

Her back still faced him, but he didn't need to see her face to know she was crying. He could hear the tears in her trembling voice.

Vincent knew, but he didn't want to really talk about it.

"I'm a fool for thinking this perfect little life I had with my husband and child could last. I was lost in the lie of our lives. It was all just a big lie. I never thought it was this fragile. I just don't understand how it could all fall apart so fast, so goddamn fast."

He stood and walked up next to her and saw the tears streaming down her face. He placed his hand on her shoulder, but she shrugged it off.

"Please don't touch me!" she snapped and wiped her cheeks. "I don't need your sympathy, and I certainly don't need your affection."

"Sorry."

She turned and in a vicious tone said, "And what do you think this is, you and me? Do you think you're some sort of hero? I'm a woman who has just seen her husband die and her son almost sexually assaulted. I've been raped and beaten since all of this began. Do you think you can help me and somehow all of that goes away? You think that we might have something, that I'll just open my legs for you?"

"Hold on a second, I was just trying to give a bit of comfort, nothing more," Vincent said, defending himself.

"No, you weren't. Men are fucking pigs. You only think with your cocks."

Vincent was in total disbelief at her outburst.

"I don't know you, and what I do, if it's true, isn't all

that impressive."

Hearing enough, he hopped away from her and grabbed his crutches. Out of the corner of his eye, he spotted Noah standing in the doorway.

She continued her emotional diatribe, but Vincent wasn't listening, he kept staring into Noah's sad eyes.

After a few minutes of yelling and crying, she stormed off. On her way out of the kitchen, she almost knocked Noah over but took no notice and raced upstairs.

Vincent hurried to Noah and asked, "You all right, little buddy?"

"Yeah."

"Sorry you had to hear that."

"I'm used to it."

"Your mommy yells a lot?"

"Especially when she doesn't have her medicine."

Then it became a bit clearer for him. "Did your mommy run out of it?"

"Yes, when we went to get stuff for my dad, she was also trying to find medicine for her emotions."

"I see."

"Do you want to play?" Noah asked.

"Um, sure, what were you thinking?"

Noah held up a deck of cards and said, "Go Fish?"

"I love that game, c'mon."

Carlsbad, CA

Karina woke to find Michael still going through items in Nicholas' office in the hopes it would clear the fog that had covered his recent memories.

"Good morning," she said, standing in the doorway.

"Hi," he replied, looking up briefly, his eyes heavy and bloodshot.

"I suppose if you found something, you would have woken me," she said as she sauntered in and knelt next to him.

"I was thinking, I remember sending him something, I just wish I could remember what. I keep looking at everything around the house, and I just know it's not here."

"You need some rest now; otherwise you're no good to us."

"Anatoly must be pulling his hair out," Michael said as he rested into the leather office chair.

"You have to ignore him. He's always been high-strung."

"So you've known him for a long time; how is it I don't remember him?"

"Did you ever meet every boss or manager a girlfriend had from work?"

Michael thought and it made sense, but when he reflected on everything—the story of the spear and its magical powers and a powerful secret organization hunting for it—he couldn't help but feel it was a fairytale. It just didn't seem legit, but again, he did remember Karina, and he was there on that ship, trying to stop Viktor. The other odd element of everything was why they were all Russians. Massive conspiracies had to be more international in scope and reach beyond one nationality. He had these questions but feared asking. He had become more trusting, but he wasn't at a hundred percent yet, and that included Karina.

"I mean it, you need to get some rest," Karina said as she tugged at his arm to get up.

"I will later, I need to keep searching, plus I'll catch some sleep on the ride to Montana later today."

"Then let me get you something to eat. You must be famished."

"That I'll take, whatever you have will work."

Karina kissed him on the cheek and left the office.

Michael couldn't get past how everything fit, and a nagging feeling kept tugging at him. Was this for real, and was the spear, if it were real, the real reason for them to have these coordinates? He had been thinking that if something so powerful existed, its hiding place would be not only difficult to find but highly protected. He wondered how they thought they could just walk in and take it.

Suddenly, an idea came to Michael. He sprang up out of his chair and raced out of the office, nearly bumping into Karina.

"Where are you off to?" she asked.

"We're not the best investigators. How about asking Nicholas' neighbors where they went? They might know or give us a clue." Michael said as he put on his gear.

"I'm coming with you," Karina said and went to go get her things.

After two hours of finding neighbors who would talk to them, a clearer picture of what had happened to Nicholas during the initial days after the lights went out became clear. Something else also became clear; they would have to leave soon. The community had slowly gathered around the helicopter, asking for help. Each attempt they made to seek assistance was met with a rifle muzzle and a firm denial. Francis and two of his team stayed at the house while the others protected the helicopter.

At each house they went to, they found people who were starting to show the signs of neglect and desperation. As they asked for information concerning Nicholas, their questions were answered with questions about how they could help them. Some people were even hostile once they were told they couldn't help them in return. Civility was gone for many of them and replaced with a hunger for survival.

Seeing how the interaction with the neighbors went, Francis warned Anatoly that the time to leave needed to be soon.

Anatoly agreed but asked for more time to sort through things.

Back at Nicholas' house, Michael, Karina and Anatoly sat to discuss the stories they had been told.

"Your brother sounds like he's cut from the same cloth," Anatoly said.

"He's a McNeil, that's for sure," Michael said.

"And from the pictures I've seen, he's also handsome like his older brother," Karina said, winking at Michael.

"You mentioned that my family has been protecting

these relics for a long time."

"Yes, the McNeil's have been protectors for many centuries."

"How is it again that I was the only one with the knowledge of the whereabouts of the spear?"

"After World War Two, General Patton, also a Knight, captured the spear from Hitler. He had heard of its power and wanted to procure it for the United States, so he immediately had a copy made and gave that to the Austrian government. The real spear was sent to its current location somewhere in the United States. One of a small team of men who took it there was your grandfather. He recorded its location and kept it secret until you discovered it. You never told us how you discovered the secret but told us it was safe."

"But someone has to have it besides me—those other men who escorted it back from Europe."

Karina looked at Anatoly, shocked that Michael wasn't piecing it all together. "They all died in a plane crash, including your grandfather."

"Those who have possession of the spear will have great power; once it leaves their possession, they soon die. Patton died not long after giving it to your grandfather and his team. They soon died after hiding it. Only they knew where it was placed. We thought it would be gone forever until you said you had discovered its whereabouts. Right after that, Viktor heard, and here we are."

"But you said Viktor did everything to get the spear, so how could I have been trying to stop him from getting it before I knew I had it?"

"Viktor has always desired to destroy the world so he may rise from its ashes and take control. His plan to cause a world war between Russia and the United States was something he was already working on; however, when he heard you knew the location of the spear, he accelerated his plan and placed his focus on obtaining the spear to ensure his dominance," Anatoly explained.

Michael cracked a smile.

"What is so funny?"

"Spears, magic, knights, it just seems like a fantasy story," Michael said.

"But a vast conspiracy, where a group gets a nuclear weapon specifically designed to emit higher gamma radiation to create the super-EMP that has paralyzed the United States, is something that happens every day. Then your president starts a nuclear war with Russia, and now several of your cities are lying in ruin from a Russian nuclear counterattack. That too is fantasy and only happens in movies," Anatoly shot back.

"But magical powers, really?" Michael smirked.

"I wouldn't have wasted my life protecting those ancient relics if it weren't so, and let's establish this, Michael, you were the one—you, my friend—who mentioned you had discovered the spear's location. That discovery led to Viktor's pushing his plans up and getting this whole thing started. You might have been able to stop them, but they moved quicker and deployed many diversions. Your government and your intelligence community failed. You even managed to get yourself in a position that found you on the ship but unable to communicate the location of the ship. The rest is history."

Hearing he might have been to blame or was the one person who helped to ignite the destructive plan made him sad. Looking back on the memories he did have from his earlier years, he knew his life had been to serve and protect. If his acknowledging the location of the spear sped up Viktor's diabolical plan, it would haunt him.

"Anatoly, you reminding him of that doesn't help. We need him only thinking about what he sent to his brother, not this playback of things that make no sense. Whatever he sent his brother might be right in front of us; it could be as simple as a token, a coin, a book..." Karina said.

"It could be anything; it's like finding a needle in a haystack. We should go find my brother and see exactly what I sent him," Michael said, his voice had dropped as he took on a more somber tone.

"Your brother left with a group of people. They had vehicles and most likely would have gone to what they considered a safe place, and from what Michael said, that would be Montana. Let's finish up here and head there," Anatoly said.

As if on cue, the sound of small-arms fire sounded outside.

All three jumped to their feet and ran towards the front door.

The door burst open, almost hitting them as Francis came running in. "We're under attack!"

"By who?" Anatoly asked.

"The community, we have to get you somewhere safe, now!"

The crack of fully automatic fire from the helicopter roared.

"Why are they attacking the helicopter?" Michael asked.

Francis took Michael by the arm and said, "Because it's a helicopter, they want to take it."

"That's our ride; we need to protect it!" Michael blurted out.

"I told them to leave and come pick us up farther away. We have to get moving!"

Michael pulled away from Francis and ran to see for himself what was happening. He ran to the end of the driveway and could see a mob of people, nearly forty, had converged on the helicopter. They were armed and returning fire.

The large twin propellers of the CH-47 Chinook began to wind up.

The situation was completely out of control. Michael could see the crew chief firing his sidearm while trying to raise the rear ramp. The slide to his pistol locked; in fear, he threw it at five men who charged onto the helicopter.

The propellers were fully engaged and the helicopter lifted off.

People on the ground continued to fire what small arms they had.

Michael watched the helicopter bank hard to the left and erratically jerked hard, its nose pointed near the ground. He now had a clear view of the cockpit and could see the men had gained access there.

Francis came out and grabbed him. "We have to go!"

"Watch out!" Michael said and pushed Francis to the ground.

The helicopter flew over just forty feet above them.

They both looked up and in shock watched the helicopter collide with the top of a house three doors down. The collision spun the helicopter three hundred and sixty degrees and into a house across the street. It slammed sideways and exploded in a fireball.

The explosion shook the ground and sent fiery debris hundreds of feet.

Michael looked up and saw the remnants of the mob coming towards them. He looked at Francis and said, "I think it's time to go."

Wellsville, Utah

Back at the house, Nicholas found several armed men standing guard. His blood boiled at the sight of them. Not frightened, he marched over and asked, "What are you doing here?"

"The mayor ordered us to come and protect you."

"Protect us from what?"

"Brock was well liked, and some townspeople are upset," the man replied.

Nicholas knew this was a lie; the mayor was letting them know they couldn't leave. "Well, we don't need you, so leave."

"Sorry, sir, we have our orders."

"It won't be necessary; they're leaving except for me."

Sophie was standing next to Nicholas and said, "I'm not going anywhere."

"And her too, so we don't need your protection."

"No one is allowed to leave until the trial is over," the guard informed him.

"Now you're telling me we can't leave?"

"No, sir, it's for your protection."

Nicholas found his temper rising to a point he'd lose it but kept his cool. He looked squarely into the man's eyes and in his mind told him where to stick it. He looked at Sophie and said, "Let's go inside."

As soon as he and Sophie came inside, Becky and Abigail rushed them. "What did the man say?" Becky asked.

"That we can't leave," Nicholas answered.

Colin walked in and said, "At least they're sticking to the same story."

"Did you manage to see her?" Becky asked.

"What about Rob?" Abigail interjected.

"Neither," Nicholas replied. He was tired and the fatigue showed on his face.

Becky took his face in her hands and rubbed his stubble-covered cheeks. "I'm sorry."

"Nothing to be sorry for."

"None of this would have happened if we had just listened to you."

"We've already discussed that; it's water under the bridge. Our focus needs to be on getting Bryn back. I fear this trial is nothing more than a formality that will lead to her execution."

"Huh?" Becky said.

Nicholas looked at her and said, "I need everyone in here. We need to talk."

Once everyone was together, he told them about their conversations with Tom and how Bryn would be executed if convicted of the murder of Brock. All expressed shock, but Frank became enraged. Marjorie, who had a tense relationship with Bryn, was upset and wanted to find a way to help her.

A car horn blared outside, pausing their group meeting.

Colin walked to the window, looked out and declared, "Hey, Nic, the mayor's here."

"Good," Nicholas said as he headed for the door.

"I'm coming with ya, boss," Colin said.

"No, stay here, get your rifle and cover me. If anything happens, take them all out and get the hell out of here. Everyone else, get ready to roll; if this goes south, we'll need to get the hell out of here."

All agreed and rushed to grab their belongings, except Colin, who took up a position behind a chair but with a clear view of the truck, the mayor, and the guards.

Nicholas had mixed feelings, seeing Chad. He was happy because he might be able to discuss the incident, and he was nervous because this could go very badly. He took a deep breath and walked up to a truck. The window was down, and sitting in the passenger seat was Chad.

Chad's face was strained with deep circles around his eyes.

"Chad, let me give you my deepest, heartfelt

condolences," Nicholas said with meaning, as he did feel truly bad for Brock's death.

"Thank you, Nicholas."

"I know why you're here, and I want to thank you."

"You presume to know why I'm here, but you're wrong," Chad said and gave Nicholas a hard look.

This was the fear he had before he went down to see Chad.

"Before you say anything else, let me tell you how sorry we are, and none of this was meant to happen, it just happened. My family and friends in there have nothing to do with this. I would like to request you remove these guards so they can move on."

"These men here are for your protection, and no one can leave. All of you will be called as witnesses in the trial."

"Chad, be reasonable, this idea of a trial is—"

"Is how we do things here. We are a good people. We opened our arms to you, and when we sent our people out to help find your lost people, one of them murdered my son. Logan told me what happened. It's disgusting, truly. My son begged her to listen, but she didn't. She just opened fire on them. Her negligence resulted in the murder of Brock and the unfortunate death of the other person in your group."

"You have to understand it from her position."

"I will, we will. Our court will be impartial and just. We will get to hear her side of it very soon. In fact, I heard she's awake and talking. Her health seems to be good enough to proceed as early as the weekend."

"That's two days away. She's been shot, she's injured.

She needs time to talk to someone, some sort of legal representation."

"She's well enough to fight two nurses and cause mayhem at the hospital. That girl is trouble, so much that we've had to sedate and restrain her."

"Chad, you wanted us to stay and now this?"

"Clearly I made an error in judgment. Consider this conversation my revocation of our invitation."

"When can I see her?" Nicholas asked.

"When the trial starts."

"Doesn't she get legal representation for this kangaroo court you're holding?" Nicholas snarled. His congenial tone was now gone. He couldn't pretend anymore, he was upset, and by what he heard from Chad, there was no negotiation available to him.

"We will appoint someone. I understand you talked with Tom this morning; he has volunteered to take her case. He's scheduled to meet her tonight."

"What about Rob's body?"

"We don't have it; we never recovered it. It's still out on the highway where the poor soul died. I'm sorry, but our concern was getting the wounded back."

"You left his body back on the road? We're going to go get it and bring it back so we can bury him."

"Like I said, Nicholas, you're going nowhere. If we have a spare team, we'll send them out to get it," Chad said with a sneer.

"You can try to stop us, but we're going," Nicholas declared.

"I can't be held responsible for what happens."

Nicholas felt like reaching into the car and pulling Chad out and beating him.

"I'd suggest you let us get him so there's no more bloodshed," Chad said snidely.

"I was hoping we could work something out, but it doesn't look that way," Nicholas said, biting his tongue for fear his own rhetoric would get him upset further to a point he may not be able to control his actions.

"Have a nice rest of your day, Nicholas," Chad said. The driver of the truck started it and revved it loudly. "And Nicholas, I feel honesty is the best policy, so make sure you prepare yourself and your group."

"For what?"

"Bryn will be found guilty, there's no doubt, so prepare your people for Bryn's execution, which will be handed down immediately following her conviction," Chad said and grinned.

The truck sped off before Nicholas could respond. He stood for a moment, stewing on the conversation. Across the street a few townspeople came by and made disparaging comments. Nicholas raised his middle finger and mouthed, "Fuck you." He turned and marched back inside the house.

"What did he say?" Becky asked.

Nicholas looked at everyone; their faces longed for news that would be promising. However, what he was about to tell them could lead to more death and a possibility that they'd never see Montana, but he couldn't allow the trial to go forward and would never let them kill her. They had to take a stand, and this was their time. "He said what I expected him to say, but what he finished with leaves us no choice. We will have to free her, and I can't guarantee the outcome of doing so."

"But what did he say?" Marjorie asked.

"He said the trial is going forward, that she would be found guilty, and her sentence would quickly follow. In a nutshell, if we do nothing, Bryn will die."

"We have to go get her," Frank declared.

"I agree," Becky stated.

"What did he say about Rob?" Abigail asked.

"They never brought him back; they left him out there," Nicholas answered.

Abigail was quickly overcome with grief and began to cry.

"Why did they leave him out there?" Marjorie asked, her demeanor cool and levelheaded, a vast departure from the more emotional approach she'd had just weeks before.

"Because they don't care," Sophie said.

"I don't understand why they would do that," Marjorie said.

"Mom, it doesn't matter why, they did it, but our biggest concern is getting Bryn," Becky said, raising her voice above some of the side chatter that was starting.

"Nic, Becky, I'm sorry, but I can't vote to help in this. I vote against it," Katherine said.

"No one has to go along, but this isn't up for a vote. I'm going to get her. If you don't want to participate, then that's fine, but you don't have a vote as to whether this happens. It's going down," Nicholas said.

"Then I don't need to sit here and listen to this insanity." Katherine stood and left the room, Evelyn in her arms.

Nicholas looked at Colin, who shrugged and said, "You know where I stand; they've got my girl. It's time to crack some skulls."

"I think we should vote on this because the consequences could affect us all," Marjorie said.

"Give me a gun, son. I'll help," Frank said defiantly.

"I need you here to defend everyone. Colin and I are going to get her. I need you back here to help ensure Becky and the others get out."

"We have to vote!" Marjorie demanded.

"Sorry, Mom, not going to happen, we're pressing forward regardless. The life and death of one of our own is at stake. We're going to get her."

"What's the plan?" Colin asked.

Marjorie sat silent now, knowing that even if they held a vote, her point of view would lose.

Nicholas pulled everyone in close and said, "The first part of my plan is a diversion, something spectacular, and from there it will be brute force, so I want everyone prepared to fight hard."

Carlsbad, CA

"Well, that was a clusterfuck!" Francis bellowed.

"Should we see if there are any survivors?" Karina asked.

"No one survived that," Michael said.

Following the battle and subsequent helicopter crash, Michael, Karina, Anatoly, Francis and two additional security men escaped down the steep embankment behind Nicholas' house. When they reached the bottom, they were cut up, bruised and unsure of where to go from there. Fortunately a park was within walking distance, and they made for that. Finding shelter along a grove of shrubs, they devised their next steps.

"You have a radio?" Anatoly asked Francis.

"I have something better, a satellite phone. I'll make the call," Francis answered as he pulled the phone out from a pocket on his tactical vest and dialed out.

Michael looked at Karina and saw a trickle of blood on her face. "You're cut," he said, pointing to her face.

She reached up and wiped it off only to have another drop of blood form on the small superficial cut. "If that's the worst following that, I'll take it."

"Well, that muddles our plan a bit."

Francis pocketed the phone and said, "A bird is en route to our location. I've turned on a tracking beacon; they should arrive in a couple of hours. I had to call in a favor, so I hope you don't mind that it's not one of ours."

"Good man, thank you," Anatoly said to Francis.

"Who has a chopper ready to go at a moment's notice, especially one that works?" Michael asked suspiciously.

"The company I work for."

"Company? You mean he's not a Knight or part of our group?" Michael asked Anatoly, concerned about having a third party involved.

"We've suffered some losses over time, so we

contracted some help," Anatoly replied.

"Can we talk?" Michael asked Anatoly.

"Say whatever you're going to say?" Anatoly responded.

"I know I hit my head hard and my memory isn't what it was, but I know that you can never trust a fucking merc."

"If you have a problem with me and my men, you can leave," Francis shot back.

A cool westerly breeze swept in, blowing trash and leaves across the park.

"You hired guns to take us? What kind of Mickey Mouse operation is this?" Michael asked.

"I told you, we have suffered many losses," Anatoly replied.

"You knew about this?" Michael asked Karina.

"You're overreacting. Francis is trustworthy; he's been with us for a while. He's a bit hotheaded but dependable."

Michael looked back at Francis, shook his head and said, "What is the name of your outfit?"

"What does it matter?"

"It matters."

"We have two hours; let's just get along, okay?" Anatoly requested, chiding both men.

Francis stood and joined his team, who were posted outside the grove.

With him gone, Michael lit into Anatoly. "You can't trust people who are hired guns. Believe me, they work for the highest bidder. What if Viktor has him on speed dial and makes him a better offer?"

"He's worked with us for quite a while; you have

nothing to be concerned about," Anatoly said in his own defense.

A swifter breeze came in. They looked up and saw the blue sky had been replaced with darkening clouds.

"A storm coming in?" Karina asked.

"A shit storm maybe," Michael joked.

"No, it looks like a rainstorm," Karina said.

Michael had time to kill, so he decided to ask some pointed questions to Anatoly. "You know everything about me; tell me, who are you?"

"Just a man sworn to defend—"

Michael cut him off and said, "None of the bullshit. Who are you? You're Russian, Karina you're Russian, and so is this guy Viktor. What's the deal with all the Russians?"

"I'm Ukrainian not Russian," Anatoly answered proudly.

"It's the same, isn't?"

"No, it is not. Viktor is a dirty Russian dog."

Karina reached over and tapped Michael on the head. "And I'm not Russian, I'm from Latvia."

"I guess it's true what they say about Americans."

"That you're all fat," Karina joked.

"Yes, and stupid." Michael laughed. "But seriously, where are the other Americans or Brits? Why is everyone from Eastern Europe?"

"There were many, but Viktor had them killed," Anatoly said sadly.

"That's tough," Michael replied.

"This is the God's honest truth, this is our last stand. If we fail, there will be no one left to stop him. He's ruthless and will murder anyone who gets in his way. He's a monster," Anatoly said.

"Well, let's make sure that doesn't happen," Michael said.

The light aroma of smoke hit their noses.

"I can't believe what's happening," Karina said, looking to the east at a thick black billowing plume of smoke.

"Looks like the fire is spreading. I wonder how many homes will be lost because of their foolishness?" Anatoly asked, his head craned, watching the heavy smoke.

"People are desperate. Things will only get worse," Michael said.

"You're right, things are only getting worse, and if Viktor gets his hands on the spear, things will never return to the way they were," Anatoly added.

Michael was also looking towards the smoke and said, "Things are never going back to the way they were, Anatoly, regardless of Viktor. The world we knew before is gone forever."

Vista, CA

"Aren't you curious how your mom is?" Vincent asked.

Noah shook his head.

"You're not worried?"

Again he shook his head.

"She's been upstairs all day and not a peep. Maybe I

should go up and check on her, plus I need a break from games."

"Can we play Rummy again when you come back?" Noah asked, excited about a new card game he had learned.

"I'll do something better, I'll teach you how to play Spades when I come back."

"Right on!" Noah cheered.

"When I'm done with you, you'll be a card shark," Vincent said as he sang the theme song from the movie *Jaws*. He exited the room and, with a single cane, walked up the stairs to the master bedroom. He was worried about her, and even though he was sure she was fine, he thought it appropriate to check in on her. If anything, she'd know someone cared, not that she'd acknowledge it. Standing outside the bedroom door, he paused, took a deep breath and tapped heavily on the door.

No reply came from inside.

He tapped louder and said, "Bridgette, you okay? You must be hungry."

Still no reply.

A wave of concern came over him as he imagined that she might have hurt herself. He now banged and said just below a holler, "Bridgette, you awake?" He tried the doorknob, but it was locked. His heart began to race as he now vividly saw her dead by her own hand inside. "Bridgette, open up!"

Silence from the other side.

His mind now saw her struggling to hold on after making an attempt on her own life and her survival depended on him. He stepped back, braced his weight on the single crutch, and lifted his good leg to get the door open.

The door swung open and Bridgette was standing there, a towel wrapped around her. "What are you yelling about?"

"I've been knocking, but you didn't answer. I was concerned," Vincent replied, his left leg still half-cocked.

"I just cleaned up a bit. The pressure in the shower is horrible, by the way," she said.

"The water tank on the hill must be running low. The house is on a gravity feed from it."

She looked at his leg still elevated and asked, "Were you going to kick the door in and save me?"

"Um, yes."

"I'm fine."

"I just thought."

"How about having some patience."

"Noah mentioned the antipsychotic drugs you were on. I've known people on them; one guy killed himself. So I guess you could say I get worried about people that are clinically depressed."

Bridgette's face went blank and her mouth hung open slightly. "My son said I was on drugs for depression?"

"Yes," Vincent answered, now worried he had compromised Noah by mentioning it.

She pushed past him and practically sprinted down the stairs while yelling, "Noah, where are you?"

From the living room, Vincent heard him reply, "Here, Mom."

She reached the living room and laid into him. "How

dare you discuss private issues with him. What I do is none of his business, do you understand me?"

"Yes, Mom."

"If you say anything like that again, I'll…" She paused when she realized the threat of punishment meant very little. "Just don't ever discuss things that are private to me."

"Yes, Mom."

"Now go upstairs, no more spending time with that man!"

Vincent began his slow descent when Bridgette reappeared, her face flush. She pushed past him then stopped a few steps up. "Leave me alone and leave Noah alone!" She stormed back upstairs and into the bedroom.

Noah sauntered slowly behind, as if each step brought him closer to a death sentence. He and Vincent shared a glance.

Vincent felt sorry for the boy and felt bad for mentioning it. He had enjoyed his day with him and was actually looking forward to an evening of fun. Noah had reminded him of the purity and innocence that still remained in the world, but his mother became a stark reminder of the world outside, unstable and psychotic.

Noah walked into the bedroom and the door slammed behind him.

Her voice bellowed right after as she chastised him.

Vincent couldn't stand it, he was tempted to storm into the bedroom and take Noah away, but he stopped short when he thought that it wasn't his business. He was her son, and he was nothing more than a stranger. He had no right to interfere, he told himself.

The yelling grew louder as he now heard her call him an 'idiot'.

Not able to listen, he cleared the remaining stairs and headed for the garage for a bottle of wine. If part of his evening was going to be spent listening to her moan, he wanted to do it half cut.

Wellsville, Utah

Nicholas and the group had drafted a plan of attack, and attack was exactly what it would be. He and Colin would make an assault on the hospital to free her in the early morning hours after Sophie and Frank set a diversionary fire on the opposite side of town using twenty gallons of their spare gasoline. The plan required an additional vehicle, and they factored in using the security's that was out front after they incapacitated them. They planned on not killing anyone if necessary, but if push came to shove, they would. Their first obstacle was the men posted out front, just how they could take them down without one of them sounding an alarm was difficult to figure out.

"Colin and I will sneak out the back and go around the house next to us. Give me five minutes; then, Sophie, I need you to go outside and lure one of them to the front door. Once he's there, you, Frank and Becky will subdue him. Colin and I will take the other two down," Nicholas said, reciting the plan he had imagined in his mind.

"You think this will work?" Sophie asked.

"I'm all ears on this one. I agree, I'd rather not kill anyone. Besides this other bullshit, these people seem okay, a bit out of whack but not your run-of-the-mill savages. Killing them has to be a secondary thing. However, the rules of engagement are wide open, and use lethal force when you have to."

"I hope this goes smoothly," Becky said.

"So do I, but what's our other option, let Bryn get tried for murder then killed? Not an option. We're a team, we stick together. This needs to go down at the cover of darkness, so let's get a bit of rest," Nicholas said.

Everyone nodded, understanding their responsibilities.

A knock on the door startled them.

Nicholas looked at Colin and motioned for him to get behind the door and attack if need be.

Once Colin got in place, Nicholas opened the door to find the last person he'd imagine seeing, Luke. "You little son of a bitch!" Nicholas cried out as he reached for Luke in a threatening manner.

"No, please, no, don't," Luke pleaded. He stood in the open doorway, alone and holding a platter of food.

"What the hell are you doing here?"

"I'm here to help you, please," Luke begged.

"Help? I remember the last time you used that word," Nicholas barked.

"Please let me explain."

Nicholas grabbed and pulled him inside while Colin slammed the door shut.

"I don't have much time because the security will suspect something if I'm in here too long," Luke said, his arms shaking as it held the platter of enchiladas.

"I should beat your ass right here and now for what you did to us. You are the cause of three people being killed; you're a lying little shit!" Nicholas yelled.

"You need my help and I need your help. The enemy of my enemy is my friend, right?" Luke said.

"How are you an enemy of Wellsville?" Becky asked.

Luke looked at everyone's deathly stares, even Marjorie glared. "It's only a matter of time before they come after me."

"What are you talking about?" Nicholas bellowed.

Luke took a deep breath and said, "The mayor wants me gone."

"If you want to leave, then fucking leave," Nicholas blasted.

"But I can't leave. I know it sounds confusing. I see where this all seems out of context. Let me explain everything, then you'll understand," Luke said, almost on the verge of hyperventilating.

"We can't believe this punk," Colin said as he stepped forward and towered over Luke.

"Just let me explain, and if it sounds like a lie, you can beat me to a pulp."

"First, how can you help us?"

"I have these," Luke said, holding up a set of keys.

"And?"

"They're keys to the hospital, every single door, and this one is the key to the east rear door. Your friend is just a few doors down from there."

"Now what do you want from us?"

"I need your help loading a truck."

"Loading a truck? Loading what into a truck?" Colin asked, highly suspicious.

Luke shifted his eyes and answered, "Gold."

"You're stealing gold from your town?" Nicholas asked.

"No, I'm stealing gold from my dad and the mayor; it's not theirs to begin with. They've been raiding banks and taking people's stuff ever since this all happened."

"What are you talking about?" Nicholas asked, interested in what Luke had to say but still wary of the boy.

"The mayor and my dad have had a racket going since this happened. They had been using their own people but found that some didn't agree. Well, those people vanished, you know, left town. Then they'd bring in new folks, convince them to stay, and then hold something over them to get them to do raids on other towns and break into banks or whatnot to steal stuff."

"So your dad and the mayor are bandits?" Nicholas asked.

"Pretty much."

"Fucking marauders disguised as clean white folk," Colin joked.

"I have to say, I don't really give a shit if they're stealing gold. Just let us go and they can steal all the gold they want."

"Those men who kidnapped you, they worked for the mayor for a couple raids until there was a falling out. They took me and my sister to hold as ransom, but Brock and his raiding parties went after them, and as you saw, that's what happens when you don't agree with the mayor—you end up dead."

"Those guys were scum and got what they deserved," Nicholas said.

"Regardless, I've made it a point to blow their cover, and now I'm in a bit of trouble. However, I'm not leaving until I get some of that gold. This is where you guys come in; I'll help you and you help me. We don't have to see each other ever again."

Nicholas looked at Colin and then his wife. "What a story, kid, but I don't think I want your help. We'll just let the legal process work here."

"You don't get it, the mayor is going to leverage your friend's life in exchange for you going out and doing his dirty work."

For Nicholas, Luke's story seemed like some teenage boy's conspiracy theory, but then he remembered hearing the mayor's argument with Chuck. "Is your dad Chuck Summers?"

"Yes."

"I don't know about all of this; it's a bit much to take in," Nicholas said.

"You need to get your friend out and leave, or you'll end up being the mayor's bitch, and when he's through with you, you'll disappear like everyone else does." Luke was still holding the enchiladas and the smell was making Nicholas hungry.

"Can someone take those things away?" Nicholas said, referring to the platter.

Marjorie took them and walked into the kitchen.

"Let's talk in private," Nicholas said and placed his hand on Luke's shoulder and walked him into the dining room. "I trusted you once and you screwed us. You have to see this is all too convenient. If I trust you and you turn on me again, I will kill you, no ifs, ands or buts."

"Mr. McNeil, I hate this place and want out; you hate this place and want out. I need help and you need help. Let's help each other."

"So what's your plan?"

Carlsbad, CA

Karina had been right; the clouds she saw were storm clouds. The winds had picked up and a cool drizzle fell from the sky.

Michael's lack of sleep had finally taken its toll. Unable to keep his eyes open, he drifted off only to be awoken by Francis kicking his foot. "Keep up, the bird is coming."

Karina and Anatoly were up and ready to leave.

Michael sat up, stretched and yawned. The nap was good but not nearly enough. He hoped to find a place to lie down on the chopper and catch up on his sleep some more.

The thumping grew louder and louder until a black Sikorsky S-70 appeared over the rooftops of the houses above.

Francis was on a radio and said, "Popping smoke." He then ran out thirty feet, pulled the pin on a smoke grenade, and tossed it onto the most open part of the park.

The helicopter swung around and made one pass before coming in and landing on top of the green smoke. The side door of the helicopter opened and a man wearing a uniform similar to Francis' stepped out. He motioned for Francis and the group to come forward.

"Time to go to Montana," Michael said to Karina.

"Good, I'm also excited to meet your brother and solve this mystery," she replied and gave him a peck on the cheek.

Anatoly shook his head, showing his disdain for their affection.

"Let's go, people!" Francis cried out.

The propellers were still thumping, making it hard to hear.

"We're not winding down, get on the bird so we can get out of here!" Francis ordered.

Michael looked at the helicopter and did a mental count in his head to ensure there would be enough seats. If he remembered right, the S-70s were civilian commercial models of the UH-70 Black Hawks, and his experience from the Army told him they'd all fit fine. He put his arm around Karina and followed Anatoly and Francis to the awaiting helicopter.

Anatoly froze when he reached the helicopter door and held his arms up.

Michael heard him yell something but couldn't make it out, but he knew something was wrong. His instincts kicked in, so he reached for his pistol but felt the cold muzzle of a rifle at the back of his head.

"Take your hand off the gun and put it into the air!"

Francis ordered.

Anatoly backed away from the helicopter, but one of Francis' men ran up and held a gun to him, the other did the same to Karina.

Several men poured out of the helicopter, disarmed Anatoly, Karina and Michael and placed them into the helicopter, and in a flash they were airborne and on their way to an unknown location with an unknown captor.

"What's going on, Anatoly?" Michael asked, yelling into Anatoly's ear.

"Just shut your mouth," Francis ordered, nudging Michael with a poke to his ribs.

The crew chief pointed to headsets hanging from the ceiling.

Michael and the others put them on.

A voice that Michael remembered came over. "Anatoly and Mikhail, so nice to see you again."

Michael spun around but couldn't see into the shadows behind him. "Who is this?" Michael asked.

"I've heard you've had some issues with your memory. You don't know how much that upsets me. How could you forget me?" the voice said as the man behind it leaned out of the shadows, exposing himself to the others.

The deep scar on his face brought back a memory from the ship and being tortured. "Viktor!" Michael exclaimed.

"You do remember me? But what I need you to remember is what you did with those coordinates. I need to know where the spear is."

"I don't know," Michael said.

"Maybe you need some encouragement," Viktor said and looked at Francis.

Francis grabbed Anatoly and punched him in the face, knocking off his headset.

Karina cried out, "No, don't hurt him."

Anatoly spit out blood and smiled. He looked at Michael and said, "Looks like I should have listened to you."

"I told you that you can't trust mercs," Michael said.

Francis gave Michael a devilish grin and punched Anatoly again.

Anatoly's head swung back, and when he brought it forward, he spit again. This time a chunk of tooth came out.

"I'm going to fucking kill you," Michael said.

Francis got in Michael's face and yelled, "Never going to happen." His heavy New York accent came out that time.

Not caring what happened and knowing he was an asset to Viktor, Michael decided to act. Francis' face was inches from his, so he head-butted him hard.

The blow sent Francis reeling backwards and into the side of the helicopter. He reached up to examine his nose and pulled his hand away to see blood on it. "You motherfucker!" he screamed and lunged at Michael.

Michael was ready; he leaned back and kicked him squarely in the chest.

Francis again flew back against the side. Angered by his beating, once again he came at Michael.

"Stop this now!" Viktor yelled.

Francis stopped just inches again from Michael, his fist

clenched, and he sneered.

Michael flinched and Francis jumped, scared he might get struck again.

"You're a dead man," Francis barked.

"One day I will die, but not by you, son, not by you," Michael chided.

Anatoly looked at Michael and began to laugh.

Francis' eyes grew wide with anger, and he lashed out at Anatoly. He jumped on him and began to pummel him.

Michael was not going to allow Anatoly to be subjected to that so he went for Francis.

Again, Viktor ordered, "Stop it! Fucking stop it, now!"

Francis stopped hitting Anatoly, and Michael let go of Francis.

Without a care, Anatoly laughed again. His bloodied mouth stretched wide and his left front tooth was now missing.

"Michael, where is the spear?" Viktor asked with his thick Russian accent.

"I fucking told you, I don't know. The beating you gave me on the ship made me lose my short-term memory. I can barely remember as far back as six months or so."

"I told you what I would do. Do you remember that?"

Michael knew he was referring to Karina. "Vaguely."

"How about I remind you," Viktor said and nodded to Francis.

Francis stood and grabbed Karina.

Michael went to move, but two other men restrained him.

With his large hands, Francis began to choke Karina.

He grunted as he applied more pressure to her slender throat.

"Leave her alone. If I knew something, I'd tell you, I swear it," Michael pleaded.

"Where is the spear?" Viktor asked.

"I don't fucking know."

Viktor nodded again.

Francis stopped choking her, but he wasn't through yet. He dragged her heaving and panting to the side door and opened it.

Cool wet air blew in and swirled around.

"What are you doing?" Michael screamed.

"I told you what I would do to her if I caught her."

"No, don't hurt her. I'll tell you everything. I will tell you everything," Michael begged.

Karina's eyes were full of fear as Francis held her next to the open door. Her dark hair whipped in the wind and partially covered her face.

Michael could see she was terrified, but she wasn't begging. She wasn't going to give them the satisfaction. The only thing that prevented her from falling thousands of feet to her death was the decision of a cold-blooded killer.

"Michael, there's nothing you can say. I keep my promises. So when I tell you that you better tell me where the spear is or I'll kill your brother and his family, you'll know I mean what I say," Viktor said and one last time nodded.

Francis looked at Karina and said, "Bye, sweet tits." He shoved her out the open door.

Karina didn't scream or cry out as she went. One

second she was there, the next she was gone.

Francis leaned out to watch his handiwork, which was his last mistake.

Michael, in a fit of anger, broke free of the two men and lunged at Francis. He grabbed him by the throat, squeezed hard and with a vicious tone said, "I told you I was going to kill you." Michael then threw him out the open door.

The two guards grabbed Michael, but he wasn't giving up without a fight. He elbowed one and wrapped his arm around the other's head and twisted, breaking his neck. He let that man drop and snatched the other and tossed him out of the helicopter.

Seeing an opportunity, Anatoly rose and attacked two more guards, but his assault was repelled easily with a rifle butt to the face. He fell back into his seat, unconscious.

Michael turned on them next. He punched one in the throat, dropping him, and the other swung his rifle but underestimated the tight confined space and hit the ceiling. Michael punched him squarely in the jaw. The full-force punch dropped the man. Michael was on a rampage and couldn't be stopped. He now knew that if he took the helicopter down, he could kill Viktor and end this insanity once and for all. He pivoted to attack the pilots, but upon turning, the copilot shot him with a Taser. The electrical volts brought him to his knees, then onto his side. He twitched as the voltage ran through his body. He heard one of the guards yell, "I got him!" just before he blacked out.

CHAPTER SIX

"All warfare is based on deception." – Unknown

Wellsville, Utah

The plan was set and Luke was going to be a part of it. It took a lot of back and forth and many hours to haggle out the details and for Nicholas to finally give his approval.

Based upon information from Luke, they needed to move quickly, and they'd be going in the early morning hours. He knew all the patrol and raiding party schedules, which proved to be beneficial to their planning and was another reason they had to move now versus wait a day or so.

All the raiding parties were deployed, and to add insult to injury for Wellsville, Chad had ordered more than normal. This put a strain on the town's security, but he was going after a big prize in Salt Lake City to the south. The more raids they completed, the larger and farther away they had to go for fresh booty; this in turn required more people. This was the real reason Chad had been pushing so hard and pulling in every passerby they came upon along the highway. His thirst for more treasure and greater spoils forced him to expand.

The plan to get Bryn was fairly cut and dry. After

subduing the three guards out front, the group would split into three.

Sophie, with the help of Luke and using a car he had acquired from his father's house, would set a large fire at a supply warehouse in the southeast part of town. This would pull many of the town's resources to deal with that.

Colin and Nicholas would take the guards' truck and head directly to the hospital to get Bryn.

Becky, Abigail, Frank, Marjorie, Katherine and Evelyn would take the Suburban, minus the trailer, and head out of town, following a route given by Luke. This route would take them overland until they were well past any checkpoints. They'd then get onto the highway and begin their trek north. Their goal was to stop at the first exit in Montana and wait for the rest to arrive.

After Bryn was rescued, they were to meet up with Luke and Sophie so they could help him load a truck he had stashed near Chad's old gravel pit.

Nicholas had all the lights turned off hours before, and the group sat in the dark, talking. This was done so the guards would believe they were asleep. Their cue to move would be when the lights of Luke's car pulled up outside.

"I'm nervous," Becky said, holding Nicholas' hand.

He leaned and whispered, "I am too, but I know we'll be all right. When you get in the Suburban go, don't look back, just drive until you get to Montana. We won't be far behind."

"I know, I just wish there was a way to solve this without all of this," she said.

"Me too, but we have even more reason to do this

after what Luke said."

"I don't trust him."

"Me either."

"Then what are we doing?"

"We're doing the same plan as before, we just have keys and hopefully a route that is good. Otherwise, we're doing almost exactly what I had worked out with Colin; it just doesn't require storming the hospital."

"I'm just worried; I can't lose you."

Nicholas gave her a kiss and said, "I love you."

"I love you too."

Headlights streamed into the house and danced along the wall.

"That must be Luke. Game time, people, let's move," Nicholas ordered.

Everyone rose and headed out the back of the house. Colin, Sophie and Nicholas went right and the others left, as the Suburban was parked along that side.

Nicholas could hear Luke chatting with the guards; then three distinct flashes and heavy thuds came from the truck.

Colin was watching and asked, "Did he just shoot those guys?"

Nicholas already had his pistol drawn but was hoping he didn't have to use it. With Luke taking the initiative, the cat was out of the bag. They'd have to go through each step killing now, especially if the word got out before they could leave.

Colin, Sophie and Nicholas raced over to the truck.

Luke saw them and said, "Hurry up."

Nicholas walked up and said, "Turn your lights out."

"Let's go, guys," Luke stressed.

"You killed them."

"So what?"

"I thought—"

"You thought wrong, pops. These guys weren't so nice, believe me."

"But—"

"Mr. McNeil, just because these guys were lily white and had conservative haircuts with the part to the side doesn't mean they were the good guys."

"You have a suppressor?" Nicholas asked.

"Yes, I do," Luke answered proudly.

While Nicholas was talking to Luke, Colin pulled the bodies out of the truck and dragged them around the rear of the house.

Sophie jumped in the car with Luke, and he said, "You ready to burn some shit down?"

"What's gotten into this guy?" Sophie asked Nicholas.

"I'll see you west of the hospital in thirty minutes," Nicholas said.

Luke acknowledged and sped off.

The rumble of the Suburban's engine caught Nicholas' attention.

Colin finished with the bodies and said, "All done."

Nicholas was fully committed now. After Luke killed those men, he was committed to not getting caught. This had to go down smoothly or it would end up being a gun battle, one he didn't want to have.

The drive to the hospital took less than five minutes. Colin parked exactly where Luke had suggested. Now they waited for the signal, an old hand-crank siren, which would sound when the fire was spotted.

"That kid had a silencer?" Colin asked.

"Yeah, I wish I had one."

"Me too."

Like an old mechanical cat screeching, the siren sounded.

Nicholas could see the orange glow southeast of them and hoped it worked to draw many people away from them.

An explosion suddenly shook the ground and let out a massive boom.

"What the hell was that?" Nicholas asked.

"That kid either had something else up his sleeve, or that wasn't intentional."

The siren continued to blare.

Nicholas and Colin ducked as several truck headlights crossed over them. People were moving, and it all seemed like they were heading in the direction they wanted.

"It looks like it's working," Nicholas said.

"I'm ready when you are," Colin replied.

"Once more into the breach, my old friend," Nicholas said and both men fist-bumped.

They jumped out of the truck and sprinted to the rear door.

While Colin provided cover, Nicholas used the key Luke described. It passed the first test when it fit, and passed the second when he heard the tumbler disengage. Nicholas pushed down on the stainless steel handle and the door clicked and opened.

"We're in," Nicholas said. He raised his rifle and tactically entered the building.

A small lantern placed next to an empty chair illuminated the hallway in a yellowish glow.

Colin followed, his back to Nicholas until they reached Bryn's hospital room.

"Going inside," Nicholas said.

Colin pivoted around so he could see both directions.

Nicholas opened the door and the light from the hall chased away the darkness. There strapped to the bed was Bryn. She looked banged up and bruised but was most certainly alive.

"What the fuck do you want?" she asked, thinking it was a guard.

"It's Nicholas. Time to get you out of here."

"It's about fucking time," she joked.

Nicholas slung his rifle and pulled out a knife and cut her restraints.

Bryn sat up slowly and swung her legs off the bed.

"You all right?" he asked.

She put her feet on the floor and stood, but she lost her balance. "Whoa."

"You're not all right. Don't worry, I got ya," Nicholas said and put her arm around his neck and his around her.

"Sorry, I'm a bit dizzy."

"No worries, you'll be safe soon," Nicholas said as her weight put stress on his side. The pain medicine he'd been taking was working, but the physical stress of what he was doing tonight would not help him heal. He quickly walked her to the door when several loud cracks echoed in the hallway.

"We got company, boss!" Colin hollered.

Their cover was blown and Nicholas was not where he wanted to be, smack dab in the middle of the hospital.

Nicholas heard yelling and screaming from down the hall and in the main part of the hospital. The gunfire had told everyone they were there.

"Go, go, go," Colin said as he pushed them along. He noticed Nicholas moving slow, so he offered, "Let me take her."

Nicholas didn't argue.

Colin slung his rifle and swooped Bryn up, cradling her in his arms. "I got ya, baby girl, you'll be fine."

Nicholas raced past him, his side on fire from the pain in his ribs. He kicked the door open and stepped out into the rear loading area. After a quick scan he called out, "All clear."

Colin came running with Bryn's weak frame bouncing in his massive arms.

In seconds they were at the truck.

A volley of single shots from a semiautomatic rifle hit the door and rear of the truck.

Nicholas turned and engaged a single guard who had followed them out. He took aim and squeezed. The bullet ripped out of the barrel and struck the man in the chest.

He fell back, his grip on the rifle firm as he fired inadvertent rounds into the air.

Colin sat Bryn in the center and sat next to her.

She opened her eyes to slits and looked at him. With a

weakened hand she took his and said, "Thank you."

"No problem," he replied. He then looked at Nicholas and hollered, "Let's go, Nic!"

Nicholas had stood watching the exit, waiting for Colin and Bryn to get settled. Hearing Colin, he got in the truck, fired it up and slammed his foot on the accelerator.

The truck's tires smoked and spun as he turned the wheel hard to the right. Nicholas was impressed with the old 1960 Ford F-250 crew cab's performance.

When they intersected with the street out front, he turned the wheel hard again to the right and put all of his weight on the pedal. "Let's see what this old girl can do!"

Vista, CA

Vincent tossed and turned, trying to get comfortable, but his stomach prevented restful sleep as it churned and gurgled. He wasn't sure if it was the wine or what he had eaten that was making him nauseous.

Unable to find comfort in any position, he sat up. The light glow coming through the blinds told him dawn was fast approaching. So unable to sleep, he decided to get up for the day.

Freshened up but not feeling any better, he made his way back to the living room and possibly another try at resting. When the light from his lantern hit the room, he found he wasn't alone. Bridgette was sitting on the couch.

"What are you doing here?" he asked, surprised to see

her.

"I couldn't sleep."

"Me either."

"I also wanted to say I was sorry."

"We definitely need to work on our communication skills," he said and made his way to the leather lounge chair next to the couch.

"Come here," she said.

"Um, no, my foot aches and my stomach is a bit upset. I think I drank too much again," he said as he dropped into the chair.

She stood and approached the chair. "I'm really sorry. I shouldn't treat you the way I do. I owe you my life, I suppose."

Vincent looked at her and cocked his head. There was something off about her. In fact, her demeanor and tone were not the same. The glow of the lantern caught her face just right, and he could see her face seemed emotionless. "Are you okay?"

"I'm fine, never been better," she said as she untied the thick white robe she was wearing.

"Ahh, what are you doing?" he asked.

"I want to thank you, personally, for saving me and Noah," she said and opened her robe, showing him she was naked.

Vincent instantly became nervous, not because a woman was about to throw herself at him, but because this was Bridgette and she might turn black widow on him in an instant. He not only couldn't trust her, he knew she wasn't in the state of mind to be making decisions that entailed intimacy. She was already on a warpath, adding sex to the equation would more than likely make everything go off the rails.

She straddled him and went to give him a kiss.

The warmth of her naked body felt good through his shorts and T-shirt, but he resisted. "Ahh, Bridgette, this is not a good idea."

"It is, trust me."

"Ahh, no, this isn't a good idea in so many ways," he pressed and pushed her away.

She disregarded his resistance and tried again to kiss him.

"Bridgette, no, seriously, this would be great. I love sex, believe me, but this complicates things, and I don't think you really want this."

"No, it's fine, trust me," she said again.

"No, it's not fine because I don't trust you," he said and pushed her harder away from him.

She stopped trying to kiss him and asked, "What's wrong with you? Are you gay?"

"God no, this, it's not right. Your husband just died two days ago."

Her face grew tense and she shoved him. With one arm covering herself she got off him and cursed, "Damn fool."

"Here's the Bridgette I know."

"What the fuck does that mean?"

"Bridgette, this is not a good idea. You don't even like me, and just yesterday you said you don't even know me. Listen, I think you're good looking, but I can't do this. I like

Noah and I want to help you, but this, what you're trying to do, that fucks things up."

"So you won't fuck me, my husband wouldn't fuck me. The man who I can get to fuck me is some fat rapist at the hospital," she yelled.

"I didn't say I wouldn't, I just can't in good conscience."

"To hell with you," she snapped and closed the robe tightly.

Vincent heard the distinct sound of pills in a plastic bottle coming from the pocket of the robe. He reached out and pulled the bottle out of her pocket.

"Give me that," she barked.

He recoiled and looked at it. "Zoloft."

"I found them upstairs; now give them to me."

"Should you be taking these?" he asked.

She quickly snatched them from his hand and yelled, "I told you to leave me alone. It's none of your business what I take or do!"

Vincent grew silent and watched her. Now he knew why she was there, now the empty expression on her face made sense, she was high on antidepressants.

"You're a fucking faggot!" she barked and stormed off.

When he heard the upstairs bedroom door close, he sighed and thought about the complicated mess he was in. A strong temptation came over him to just leave. He hated drama and she was the queen of it. He could see how having her around put him at risk. She was a ticking time bomb and you never knew when she'd blow. Her problems were becoming a major liability for him, and he began to

THE DEFIANT: AN UNBEATEN PATH

question his desire to help them.

Wellsville, Utah

"Where are they?" Nicholas stressed.

Sophie and Luke had missed the rendezvous time by almost two hours.

Bryn mumbled something unintelligible in her sleep.

"Sounds like she's having a good dream," Colin said.

"The sun will be up soon. I don't know how long we can hold out," Nicholas said.

They had gotten out of town and were waiting on a long gravel road a mile outside of the gravel pit.

"Do you suppose Luke screwed us again?" Colin asked.

"I guess it's possible, but for what, Sophie?"

"Huh?" Bryn mumbled and lifted her head.

"Just sleep," Colin said.

Bryn opened her swollen eyes and looked around. She blinked heavily and shook her head. "My head is killing me."

The faint glow of the early dawn was making an appearance to the east.

"How's your arm and shoulder?" Colin asked.

More awake, she sat up and replied, "Sore. Um, what's this about Sophie?"

"She's late," Nicholas said.

"Late, why?"

"I don't know, but I'm officially worried," Nicholas said.

"We have to go find her, then," Bryn flatly stated.

Nicholas pulled out his gold pocket watch and checked the time. "Hmm, easily two hours late."

"We can't leave her. Let's head back," Colin said.

"Head back and find us all under arrest, we can't do that. We'll never make it within a hundred feet of Sophie before the light is up if she's been taken. But I have an idea," Nicholas said and started the truck. He sped off towards the gravel pit.

"Just as Luke said," Nicholas said and handed a pair of binoculars to Colin.

They had pulled off the road and taken up a hide position two hundred yards away from the gravel pit's entrance.

Colin peered through and confirmed what Nicholas had seen. "Yep, only two guards. How strange?"

"Why is it strange to use only two people to guard a pile of rocks?" Bryn asked. "And why are we even at a fucking gravel pit when we should be finding Sophie?"

Nicholas looked and saw the eastern sky had brightened even more. He heard Bryn but was focused on removing the two guards now.

"The sun will be up in thirty minutes, no more time to waste. I'll take the guy on the left, you the right," Nicholas said as he put his AR-15 into his shoulder and aimed for his target.

"Roger that," Colin replied and took aim with his rifle.

"What's so strange?" Bryn asked again.

"There's not just rocks in there, there's also gold," Nicholas replied to Bryn, never looking away from his optics. "You got your man?" he asked Colin.

"Yep."

"On the count of three—one, two, three," Nicholas said.

Nicholas and Colin fired within a tenth of a second of each other. Their aim was true, as both men dropped to the ground.

Through his optics, Nicholas continued to scan for other targets, but none showed.

"Good shot," Nicholas said and got up. "Jump in the bed. I want you able to start shooting as we bust our way through," Nicholas ordered as they all made their way back to the truck.

Colin got in the bed and placed his rifle on the roof of the cab.

Just before getting in, Nicholas looked at him and said, "Let's go get some gold."

Bryn took a hold of Nicholas' arm before he could get into the truck and asked, "What we doing?"

"We're going back to rescue Sophie, but I'm not going empty-handed."

"You're going to buy her back?"

"Sort of, consider the gold leverage," Nicholas said as he tossed his rifle in the cab. He looked at Bryn and said, "Now get your skinny ass in the truck."

Vista, CA

The restless night coupled with the brief encounter with Bridgette left Vincent exhausted to the point he slept in later than usual.

At first he thought the sound of the garage door opening was in his dreams, but when the SUV engine roared to life, he knew he wasn't dreaming. Someone was stealing his vehicle.

He tossed off the blanket and began to race as fast as a person can with a bandaged broken foot. Along the way he grabbed his pistol and made for the front door. He was too late to catch them at the garage, but he hoped he'd be able to catch them at the gate.

He cleared the front door and jumped off the deck, landing on his good foot. At the gate, like he thought, was the SUV, but the person unlocking it wasn't just anybody, it was Bridgette.

She turned and saw him coming. "Stay away from me!"

"Bridgette, you're not taking my vehicle, it's that simple!" he called back as he moved closer and closer to her.

She fiddled with the keys but was having a hard time finding the one to unlock the gate. Frustrated, she gave up and went to get back in.

He was now feet away. His options were limited, but the thought of shooting her popped in his mind.

Noah screamed.

"Shut up!" she yelled back then slammed down on the

accelerator and busted through the wrought-iron gate with one attempt.

Vincent could not let her leave with his vehicle. It was his lifeblood, and without it, he had no quick way to get to Idaho. He took aim on the rear tire and squeezed.

The bullet hit its mark, causing the tire to explode; however, she didn't slow down. He took aim on the right rear tire and squeezed, but this time he missed.

She was getting farther away but couldn't get too far, he thought.

"Fuck!" he screamed as he watched her accelerate faster.

She came to the main road, but with her excessive speed and the complications caused by the flat left rear tire, she lost control of the vehicle, slamming it into the ditch.

The crunch and scream of twisted metal told him the vehicle had taken some serious damage.

The horn blared but stopped after a few seconds.

His foot was throbbing with pain, but he moved as fast as possible towards the SUV.

The passenger door opened. Noah got out and walked towards him.

"You okay?" Vincent asked.

Noah nodded and said, "My mom is hurt."

Vincent came to the passenger side and looked in. There he saw Bridgette conscious, bleeding badly from her head and face, but pointing a pistol at him. He immediately jumped back just as she pulled the trigger.

"I'll kill you!" she screamed.

"Don't do this, Bridgette. Please, you're making a

mistake."

"I'll fucking kill you!"

"Noah, go back inside. I don't need you to see this," Vincent warned.

"What are you going to do to my mom?" Noah asked a look of concern for his mother written on his face and in the tone of his voice.

"Nothing, but I can't have her shooting at me."

"Mom, please stop shooting, please!" Noah cried.

"Baby, come to Momma. Don't listen to him."

"Noah, your mom is sick. Don't go near her just yet."

"You shut up, you hear me, you shut the hell up and leave my boy alone!"

"Bridgette, you're more than welcome to leave and go home, but you're not taking my vehicle, it's that simple," Vincent said as he sat crouched next to the right rear tire, his pistol firmly in his grip.

"Honey bear, come help Momma get out of this car," Bridgette asked, her tone softer.

Noah stepped closer but stopped when Vincent motioned him to.

"What's wrong, Mom?"

"I'm stuck. The door is crushed against my side and the seatbelt is stuck," she answered.

"Bridgette, I can help, but you have to promise not to shoot me," Vincent said.

"You stay the hell away from me!"

"I won't hurt you, I'll just free you, and you can go on your merry way."

"Ahh, damn!" she cried out.

"Momma?" Noah whined.

"Come here, baby, I need you."

Noah stepped closer, but Vincent this time held him. "No, not until we make sure she won't hurt you."

"I hear you. I won't hurt my boy, let him go, now," she said and pulled the trigger.

Glass from the right rear passenger window rained down on their heads.

"Stop shooting, you crazy fucking bitch!"

"Fuck you," she screamed and shot again.

Noah cried out, "Stop it, Momma, stop it!"

"I'll stop shooting, just come and get me out," she begged.

"Don't, Noah," Vincent said.

He pulled away and yelled, "She's my mother!" He walked up to the passenger front door and looked in. "I'm here, Momma."

"Climb in, baby, help me."

Vincent didn't trust her not to do something erratic, but what were his choices? He could jump up and put some lead in her, but then what? He had to trust she wouldn't hurt her own son.

"Can you get it, sweetie?" she asked, referring to the seat belt.

"I can't."

"Noah, I have a knife inside the glove compartment; use it to cut the seatbelt," Vincent recommended.

Noah did as he suggested and seconds later she said, "Thanks, baby, now help pull me out."

Vincent skirted away towards the rear of the vehicle

and took up a position.

Slowly Noah pulled her out and onto the ground.

She grunted when she hit the ground. "I think I broke my leg or worse."

"Momma, it's your leg," Noah squealed and pointed at the bloody bone protruding out from her left leg.

"Oh no, I broke my leg and my face. How bad is my face, baby?" she asked Noah as her trembling hand examined the deep laceration on her forehead and the even deeper and longer one on the left side of her head. Blood was everywhere as it freely streamed from her wounds down her face and onto her chest. She looked down at her leg and placed her shaking hand on the thick bone that stuck out of her femur. She cringed and began to sob when she touched the bloodied white mass as if her sense of touch made it a reality. "What have I done?" she moaned.

Noah hugged her and also cried.

Vincent was at his breaking point over the drama and wanted nothing more than to walk away, but he couldn't. "If I step out to help, promise me you won't shoot."

"Leave us alone," she sobbed.

"Your leg is broken, let me help."

"I said leave us alone."

"Great," Vincent mumbled under his breath.

"My life is shit, ahhh!" she screamed out.

"Mommy, let him help you, please. He can make it better," Noah begged.

All she could do was focus on how pathetic and sad her life was. She rocked back and forth, repeating over and over how her life was shit.

"Mommy, please!" Noah pleaded with tears flowing down his face.

"Oh, honey, I'm so sorry. I am so, so very sorry for the life I gave you. I didn't mean to be like this. It's not my fault; it's how I was made," she cried as she petted his face. With each swipe she smeared thick blood on his tender face.

"Mommy, stop talking. We can make it better," Noah said and tried to get her to move.

"Noah, I can help, but you have to tell me if she has the gun," Vincent asked from his hide position.

Upon hearing that, she snapped out of her trance, grabbed the pistol from her lap and screamed, "Don't you come near me, don't you dare!"

"Bridgette, I can help, but this is becoming a real bore for me. Either you can sit here and die, or I can patch you up and make sure Noah is safe," Vincent said calmly.

"You can't make my baby boy safe, no one can. This world is cruel and he shouldn't see the harsh brutality and inhumanity of it. I'm just so sorry that I wasn't there to stop those people, but I can make it all better. I can put an end to it, I can, baby, there's a better life up in heaven," she sobbed and put the pistol under Noah's chin.

Hearing her words, Vincent knew she had officially gone mad. He had to act and act now. He spun around to see her with the pistol stuck under his chin and Noah frozen in fear.

"Please, Mommy, don't."

Out of the corner of her eye she saw Vincent had emerged.

Vincent leveled his pistol at her and began to squeeze. Time slowed down for him as every second moved like minutes.

She pulled the pistol away from Noah and placed it under her chin and yelled, "To hell with it all!" She pulled hard on the trigger; the pistol fired one round deep into her skull, blowing the top of her head off. Blood and brain splattered against the white SUV.

Noah cried out in terror, "No!"

Even for Vincent the scene was horrific. His heart didn't go out to Bridgette though he felt for her internal pain; it went to Noah, who was now an orphan. In a matter of days he had lost his father and mother. Vincent couldn't imagine the trauma of witnessing your parent kill themselves, it was all too much.

Noah clung to her limp body with no regard for the volumes of blood that spilled down on him. He sobbed uncontrollably at her death.

Vincent understandably had lost his situational awareness due to the tense situation and suddenly felt the need to look around. He feared their loud altercation would draw onlookers even in this rural setting. He needed to get the SUV out of the ditch and back into the compound. "Noah, let's get your mom back inside so we can clean her up."

Noah ignored him and continued to cry.

"C'mon, buddy, we have to get off the road."

Noah looked up, his face covered in blood and tears.

"Okay?" Vincent asked, his hand out to help him up.

With his sleeve he wiped away some of the tears and

blood. He nodded and grabbed Vincent's hand.

"Let's get her back," Vincent said, putting his arm around Noah's shoulders.

Needing the affection, Noah embraced him tightly and cried again.

Vincent looked down at the bloody scene. In his mind he was thinking what an unnecessary mess it all was, but a cold part of him was happy she was gone. He would never admit that to anyone, but she was troubled and what demons she was fighting would have brought harm to them all.

He hugged him tightly and said, "I need you to go back and make sure the gate is open."

Noah nodded but wouldn't let go.

"Hey, buddy, we need to get off the road before any bad people show up."

"Okay," he replied and took off running towards the gate.

Vincent looked back at the scene and grumbled, "What a fucking mess."

Wellsville, Utah

When Nicholas, all alone, pulled up to the first checkpoint on the west side of Wellsville, the guards found him whistling an old show tune.

The guards raised their rifles and ordered, "Out of the truck! On the ground!"

Nicholas was feeling cocky; he lifted his hands off the steering wheel and said, "Gentlemen, you seem to know who I am, good. This is what you're going to do. Get on the radio and contact Mayor Chad, tell him Nicholas McNeil has his gold, all of it, and I want my friend Sophie back."

"Get out of the vehicle!" a guard hollered.

Nicholas looked at him and asked, "Are you deaf, dumb or both?"

The guard came towards him when the second man yelled, "Leave him, I'll call the mayor."

As Nicholas waited, he took in a deep breath, enjoying the crisp air. He also was making a mental note of where he was and what he was doing. His move to get Sophie was a risky one, but he couldn't think of anything else. Trying another armed raid would most likely fail, so he went for the one thing Chad found value in above all else. The one part of the equation he didn't know was if Sophie was even there. It was all an assumption.

The second guard got off the radio and stepped up to Nicholas. "The mayor wants you to come see him at his office."

"Not going to happen, tell the old cripple to come here," Nicholas said.

The guard took his handset and called again.

Nicholas hadn't put much thought into his own life when he made the decision to do this swap. It had just come naturally to him. Now as he waited for Chad to come, he began to think of Becky and Abigail. He loved them so much and wanted nothing more than their safety and happiness. He then thought about Chad and Brock, he remembered the conversation where Chad told him about his success and how all of his children had fled Wellsville but one, Brock. He was sure Chad had the same wants for his children as he did, so would Chad take this deal or would he be hell bent on exacting revenge? This gave him pause, the confidence he had before began to crumble. What if Chad cared more about justice for his son than all the gold in the world?

Two cars raced his way.

He was sure it was Chad and some men.

"Get out of the car," the first guard ordered, his rifle stuck near Nicholas' face.

Suddenly, Nicholas began to fear that he had made a mistake.

"Out now," the guard barked.

"Hold on, give me a second," Nicholas replied and stepped out, making sure his hands were in clear view.

The two cars came to a screeching stop.

The driver of the lead car got out, opened the trunk and pulled out Chad's wheelchair. He unfolded it and took it to the passenger-side door, which Chad had opened.

Chad threw his body into the chair and quickly whisked his way over to Nicholas.

"Hmm, I count six guys, not including you," Nicholas said.

"You certainly play a deadly game, Mr. McNeil, a very deadly game."

"I have to ask because I noticed this on day one. Did you steal all of the operational vehicles from people who needed them?"

"So I see you listened to the lies of Luke Summers."

"Lies, really? He told me there was as much gold at your old gravel pit as Fort Knox and you know what? He was right," Nicholas mocked as he pulled out a Gold Eagle and flipped it to Chad.

The coin landed in Chad's lap. He snatched it up and looked at it carefully.

Seeing Chad's reaction, Nicholas turned to the guards individually and asked, "Are you aware of all the gold he has stolen? You? Are you aware?"

Chad wheeled to within inches of Nicholas and said, "Walk with me."

Nicholas smiled; the fear that had brewed began to wane. "Sure."

Chad wheeled twenty feet away and stopped; he spun around and asked, "What do you want?"

"My friend, Sophie, you have her."

Cocking his head, Chad said, "I don't know who you're talking about."

"Now you're lying."

"I don't know who you're referring to. I see you freed your other friend, and you made a mess out of one of my warehouses and killed more than a few of my people."

"Quit screwing around, Chad."

"I'm not."

"I know this tactic, stall while you send other guys to the pits, but you won't find them. We moved it; we spent all morning moving case after case after case of gold."

Chad's forehead furrowed and his lips pursed. "Damn

you."

"Where's my friend?"

"She's in town. We caught her and that punk kid."

"Bring her to me and I'll tell you where you can find your gold."

Chad's temples pulsated as his temper grew. "Fine," he barked and turned around. "Have Logan bring the girl and the boy."

"Boy?"

"Yes, you take him or no deal."

"I don't want that kid, he's the entire reason you and I are having this conversation."

"I want him gone, but I have to play it safe because of politics. The girl and boy for my gold, that's the final deal."

Not wanting to argue anymore, Nicholas gave in. "Deal."

Vista, CA

Bridgette had been wrapped in several white sheets and a thick dark brown duvet cover. Vincent had done this to minimize the gory look of the blood-soaked sheets.

Noah had requested she be buried up on the hill next to Vincent's favorite spot in the avocado grove. Vincent had shared with him how he enjoyed the three-hundred-and-sixty-degree views from there and that it felt like he was on top of the world. This appealed to Noah, and Vincent was willing to give him anything he wanted.

Vincent's foot was in intense pain and he was beginning to think he might have rebroken it. However, he made a promise to Noah and he was going to fulfill it, pain or not.

With her body in a wheelbarrow, Vincent pushed her up the hill. Each agonizing step was worse than the last. He could feel the bones grinding in his foot, and there was no doubt now he had done some damage to it.

Noah walked behind the funeral procession with two shovels in hand.

Like Vincent's previous trips to the top, for each normal stride it took him three. When they finally reached the top, he was sweating profusely and his foot was radiating so much pain he found it hard to stand.

Seeing how much pain Vincent was in, Noah said, "Your foot hurts bad, doesn't it?"

"Yeah, real bad."

"I'll dig my mom's grave, you sit down and rest," Noah suggested.

Sucking up the pain as Marines do, Vincent said, "It's all right, I'll help."

"No, I can do this," Noah replied sternly.

Vincent could see he was determined so he let him begin while he got off his feet.

The midday sun was high above them when Noah tossed out the last shovelful of dirt. His clothes were soaked with sweat and his face had dirt stuck to his moist skin. He climbed out of the hole and looked at Vincent.

"I'm sorry I wasn't any help, but it didn't look like you needed it," Vincent said, trying to put on a happy face. The pain had gotten worse in his foot and he was having a hard time focusing.

Noah looked proudly at the torn skin and blisters on his hand and said, "You hurt your foot again because of my mom. It's okay if you don't do anything."

"She's too heavy for you to put in the hole," Vincent said as he got to his knees.

Not paying attention to Vincent, Noah grabbed the foot end of the duvet and pulled. He strained but it barely moved.

Walking over on his knees to avoid standing, Vincent grabbed the head and pushed.

Together they placed her in the three-foot-deep hole.

Without taking a break, Noah picked up the shovel and began to toss the dirt on top of his mom's body.

Vincent, still on his knees, took the other shovel and began to help.

Filling a hole is always easier than digging one, and with help, the time was cut in half. When the hole was full, they both patted it down with the backs of the shovels.

Noah walked to the wheelbarrow and took out a wooden cross he had made. He stepped to the head of the grave and stabbed the ground with it. Using the back of the shovel, he hammered it in.

When he was done, he gathered up the shovels and placed them back in the wheelbarrow. He looked at her grave then took in the view.

"Do you want to say anything?" Vincent asked.

"I love you, Mom, rest in peace."

"You're a man of few words like me."

"Can you take care of me?"

The question broke Vincent's heart. "Of course I'm going to take care of you."

"I wasn't so sure; I thought it best to ask. My mom use to say if you're not sure, ask, there is nothing wrong with getting clarification."

Still on his knees, Vincent laughed and said, "Those are very wise words."

"Are we going to stay here?"

"Ahh, I was thinking we should get on the road tomorrow."

"Where?"

"I was thinking of taking you to your family in Oklahoma."

"What about your foot?"

"Oh, um, I think I rebroke it, but I don't think we can stay here any longer. I fear the people from the cities on the coast will start migrating out here. I want to try our luck on the road."

"Okay."

Vincent hopped up on his good foot and stood. He cringed in pain just from his foot lightly touching the ground.

"Can you teach me to drive?"

Vincent laughed and said, "Sure, it's important you learn now."

"What about shoot a gun? Can you teach me to shoot like a Marine?"

"Wasn't I just saying that you were a man of few words?"

"Can you?"

Vincent looked at the grave then at him and said, "Yeah, I sure can. It's time for you to learn that as well as driving. I also think we need to get you schooled up on some other lifesaving skills. This world we're in is a tough one."

"It's about being smart, right?"

"Smart to a point, it's more about being capable and willing."

"Can you teach me everything you know?" Noah asked.

"I sure can."

Noah stepped forward and hugged him. "Thank you for saving me."

And right there, in those words on his special spot, Vincent knew his mission, knew the reason God spared his life.

Wellsville, Utah

The wait for Sophie and Luke was almost unbearable. All he could think of was Becky and Abigail. He prayed they were safe. Curious as to the time, he pulled out his watch and pushed the button to open the cover. As he closed it, the watch slipped out of his hand and hit the pavement.

"Damn," he cried out as he picked it up. The glass face

was unhurt, but the gold metal back had popped off. He picked it up and dusted it off. When he went to snap it back on, he saw something interesting. Etched into the inside back cover was a series of numbers. At first he thought it was a serial number, but as he examined it closer, he knew it wasn't that, it looked more like coordinates. The inscription read 35.878241, -97.413379.

"Here they come," a guard yelled.

"Finally," Nicholas muttered. He snapped the back on his watch and pocketed it.

The car stopped behind the other two, and two men exited the front. They opened the rear doors and Sophie and Luke stepped out.

When Sophie saw Nicholas, she smiled from ear to ear.

He could only imagine how frightened she must have been.

Luke didn't know what to expect and fear still gripped him.

The guards walk them to Chad and held them.

"Here they are. Where is my gold?"

"I'll take you."

"Tell me where it is," Chad insisted.

"That's not going to happen, follow me with one of your goon cars. I'll take you right to it; that's my final offer."

"Okay," Chad barked and wheeled himself around.

"I won't be getting out at the next stop, so let me say goodbye here and thank you for your hospitality."

Chad ignored him and wheeled away.

Nicholas looked at Sophie and Luke. He gave her a big

smile and asked, "You okay?"

"How's Bryn?"

"She's good, safe and sound."

She walked over, gave him a hug and said, "I knew you'd come for me, I just knew it."

"I remember how confident you were when we had that conversation in the kitchen."

"And I told you how much of a good guy you were. I was right, thanks, Nic."

"What about me?" Luke asked.

"You're coming with us. It's not my idea; you were part of the deal I struck with the mayor."

Luke looked apprehensive. He knew how Nicholas and the group felt about him, he just hoped they could find it in their hearts to forgive him, and he hoped his help freeing Bryn would give him some points.

"Let's go get the others and head north. We have a long drive ahead of us."

When Nicholas turned the engine over, he felt like a weight had been lifted. His ploy had worked and he had his entire group with him. If he had failed, he would have been haunted by it. Feeling almost giddy, he put the truck in gear and headed towards the pickup point.

CHAPTER SEVEN

"There is a time for departure even when there's no certain place to go." – Tennessee Williams

Intersection of California Highway 86 & 76

When Vincent woke that morning, he found Noah staring out the window towards the avocado grove. He had been a big help with preparing her body and digging the grave itself, more than Vincent would have expected from a seven-year-old that had lost his parents and witnessed his mother commit suicide.

Vincent was sure his short life had already been marred by trauma and emotional pain, so he was going to do his best at being a guardian and teacher. Being responsible for a young child was something he never imagined he'd be doing at his young age, but here he was.

The SUV was damaged but still operational. It wasn't in the best-looking shape, but it would get them out of there and to their next place, hopefully a place they could call home.

After making breakfast and taking enough painkillers to numb an ox, Vincent sprang the idea of leaving on Noah. They discussed where specifically and Noah made the choice of Oklahoma. He had family and his mother

214

would have wanted it.

Noah was excited to get on with his life and the thought of traveling sounded thrilling. So with a full belly and newfound inspiration, the two set out.

Leaving the compound earlier that morning was bittersweet for Vincent. The place had been a point of dramatic change in his life. He had been taken in there by a loving family who helped him and then departed. That experience of being surrounded by such a wholesome family unit made him long for home. Then he met a new family, but that experience was vastly different. Where Roger's family was stable, Bridgette's wasn't. Where Roger's family expressed their love openly, Bridgette's expressed anger and depression; two families, two different experiences. One cared for him, the other almost killed him. In the end he had discovered who he would become. So often a person never truly knows or embraces what life throws at them. Vincent not only embraced it, he snuggled it. He had a purpose that was greater than him, and there was nothing better than that.

He pulled up to the stop sign at the intersection of Highways 86 and 78 and made a full stop. He looked over at Noah and asked, "Which way? Left takes us north to Interstate 10, or right, we stay on Highway 78."

"You want me to decide?" Noah asked with a smile.

"This is our first lesson for today."

"Um, go right."

"Right it is," Vincent said and made the turn. He

applied pressure to the makeshift accelerator he'd made for his left foot and headed into the morning sunrise, with Noah by his side.

CHAPTER EIGHT

"Always mystify, mislead and surprise the enemy if possible." – Stonewall Jackson

Outside Whitefish, Montana

Their journey had finally come to an end when they pulled in front of Uncle Jim's ranch house. Nicholas had never been to the house, but Becky had many stories of fun times there. The large log-framed home was positioned perfectly, overlooking the Flathead River, tucked in between towering evergreens. Nicholas hadn't envisioned this type of setting, as the property had always been referred to as a ranch. He pictured rolling green fields with cattle, but this was the opposite. Most of the property was heavily wooded save for several acres that had been cleared.

"Is it safe?" Colin asked.

"We're safe from assault but not harsh words," Becky replied from the backseat.

Nicholas turned and clarified, "Uncle Jim doesn't like visitors and especially dislikes uninvited ones."

Colin laughed.

"He's serious; expect to hear a lot of yelling, bellyaching and groaning," Becky said.

"Maybe I'll stay out here until you clear things up."

Nicholas heard the trailer door open and in the

passenger-side mirror saw Abigail and Luke step out. Seeing Luke infuriated him, but they had made a bargain and Nicholas was good to his word; however, he never promised to be civil to the boy. What angered him the most was how Abigail had taken a liking to Luke; the only thing that could be worse is if they truly became an item. This was something he would ensure wouldn't happen.

"You ready, Becky?" Nicholas asked.

"Being yelled at by Uncle Jim will actually be the highlight of the trip," Becky joked.

Nicholas looked at the house for any signs of life. He was surprised Jim or his wife, Crystal, hadn't stepped outside to see who dare pull up to their house.

"Do you think anyone is home?" Nicholas asked Becky as they stepped away from the vehicle.

The first thing that hit Nicholas was the strong aroma of pine. The air was crisp and fresh and the sky was a brilliant blue. He loved the mountains, and it had been a long time since he'd been anywhere similar.

Abigail ran up next to them and asked, "Can I come to?"

Nicholas turned to make sure Luke wasn't joining her. "Of course, but not the little shit."

Abigail returned his comment with a frown and replied, "I'm not happy about what happened before, but he was only doing so to save his sister. I can respect that. I'd do the same if I were him."

"Whatever," Nicholas replied with a sneer.

"Oh, look, there's some smoke coming from the chimney," Becky said, a smile gracing her face, knowing that her uncle was home.

"A fire this time of year?" Abigail asked.

"Maybe they're cooking a big breakfast," Nicholas said.

All three cautiously made their way to the front door. They cleared the large stairs and stepped onto the gray weathered wood deck.

Nicholas peered in through a large window next to the front door but couldn't make anything out.

Becky took his hand and squeezed it.

He knew she was nervous. Over his shoulder he saw his group; Colin now stood outside the Suburban laughing with Bryn, who must have been telling one of her now famous jokes. Sophie had wandered away and was fascinated by the large softball-sized ponderosa pine cone she had found. Frank and Marjorie, who had found greater respect for each other over the long journey, watched them with apprehension. Katherine was scarred from the loss of Proctor, but her purpose in life had turned to Evelyn and her well-being, and finally Luke, who stood tense like a statue with his arms folded. Nicholas knew the boy was afraid and that his selfish actions before weren't malicious in their intent to harm others, but it would take a while for trust to be built between the two.

The long journey took a serious toll on them. Lost were Proctor and Rob, taken before their time, but also lost was any hope that people would act humanely. Wellsville had its laws and rules, the streets were clean and tidy, and the system worked, but it too was flawed. It showed that no matter how many laws are written, the emotion of mankind shapes and affects their outcomes for personal needs.

Now that they had arrived in Montana, they felt hopeful but more skeptical because of their hard journey. What lay ahead of them was promising, and for the first time in a while, Nicholas felt if he could guide the course, they might make it. He smiled at his defiant few, happy to be with them. In such a relatively short period of time, he'd found a place in his heart for them all; they might disagree, bicker, and fight, but they also laughed, cried and felt connected. These people had become his family. No one was better than the next and all had their value. It wasn't a perfect group, but he was grateful he had a group. Feeling satisfied, he turned back to the large alder-wood door and knocked.

Nicholas and Becky turned to each other when they heard heavy footsteps coming towards the front door.

"Any bets on what Jim will say first?" Nicholas asked.

"If it's Crystal, she'll say something like *oh my* or *oh dear*." Becky chuckled.

"Right, that's the polite way of saying *oh shit*," Nicholas joked.

The heavy deadlock unbolted and the handle turned.

Nicholas gulped heavily and his pulse raced in anticipation of dealing with Jim. When the door opened partially, his jaw dropped at who was standing there. "Michael, what are you doing here?"

The door then opened fully and another man appeared. "Hello, Nicholas, my name is Viktor. I believe you have something that's mine."

EPILOGUE

Outside Oklahoma City, Texas Federation

"Whoa!" Alexis exclaimed.

"It's a crazy story, isn't it?" Abigail asked.

Alexis jumped up and ran into Samuel's office.

"Where are you going?" Abigail asked, curious as to why she'd jump up and run off.

"It's true, your story?" Alexis asked from Samuel's office.

Abigail followed her and replied, "Some of it I remember, other parts I was told."

Alexis was quickly picking up one framed photograph after another until she found the one she was looking for. "Here, this is him, isn't it?"

"Who?"

"Right there, the man next to Daddy, that's Noah Vincent." Alexis cheered as if she had found a prize.

Abigail studied the photograph and said, "It is. I haven't seen him in years, but yeah, that's him. He and your dad were in the legislature together."

"So his dad was that old man who smoked a pipe; I remember meeting him at the same time I met Noah Vincent. I can still remember that because I thought the smoke smelled so good, like sweet cherries."

"You have a great memory," Abigail said.

"Unlike my great-uncle Mike," Alexis said with a smile.

"Honey, you seem way too happy," Abigail said, finding it odd that Alexis found the story more entertaining than it should have been.

"I knew Daddy was important, but our family history is very cool. I don't mean to sound so cheesy, but it's exciting."

"I wouldn't describe it as exciting in the terms you're using; that takes away from what happened."

"I know, I just never knew we were all so connected. Also, how is it you're telling Noah Vincent's story?"

"Tomorrow, let's continue tomorrow."

"Aw."

"There's good reason."

"Mom, I don't mean to sound so thrilled, it's just that I know some of what happens. I mean, the bit about the spear is just bunk."

"I'm just telling you the story as I heard it or I saw it, nothing more."

Alexis looked at her watch and said, "I'm gonna go meet up with Timmy."

"That's fine, but no telling Timmy what I told you. He doesn't know about this stuff."

"Or maybe he just hasn't told me yet."

"Your uncle doesn't know either. This is our secret; you have to promise," Abigail pressed, her tone serious.

"I promise."

"No fingers crossed?"

"I swear, Mom, I won't say anything. Can I take the phone and show him Luke's picture?"

Abigail thought for a moment and said, "I don't see why not."

"Great, love you, Mom." She kissed Abigail on the cheek and raced out of the house. Just as she hit the screen door she hollered, "Love you, Mom."

When the door slammed shut, Abigail walked further into the office and peered out the window to ensure Alexis wasn't coming back. Seeing her racing down the driveway gave her a smile. Her daughter had been raised in a harsher world than hers at her age, but she was still a good, decent and sweet girl. It had helped that she and Samuel had shielded her against some of the realities of life, but Alexis was a gentle person at her core.

Retelling all the stories that connected to her life made her feel melancholy. She thought Alexis' response was a direct result of her being too protected. This innocence made her incapable of grasping the enormity of what she had been told. This made her question whether Alexis was truly ready for the truth about who their family was and what her destiny held. She decided to not make any decisions just yet but allow it to marinate. Eventually she wanted to disclose it all, but then again, maybe it wasn't necessary.

Like Alexis, she glanced at the photographs. All of them had been taken many years after the events. She only had a few possessions from that time; the phone was one. The second was hidden away in a special place. In fact, she hadn't thought about it until she'd told the story today. Curious to see it again, she walked outside and towards the far end of the property; there she came up on a wrought-iron fence enclosure. Inside were several thick granite gravestones, all in a line, standing three feet in height. She unlocked the gate and stepped inside. Her eyes began to read the stones from left to right: Nicholas McNeil was inscribed on the first, Rebecca McNeil on the center stone, and Samuel Becker on the last. She stared at Samuel's for a bit and whispered, "I miss you."

She stepped in front of Nicholas' stone and knelt. In front of it, a small urn stood on a granite pedestal. She grabbed the cold brass urn and turned it counterclockwise until it unscrewed from its base. Setting it aside, she looked at the keyhole that was hidden beneath it. Reaching in her pocket, she removed a long slender gold key and inserted it into the keyhole and turned left until she heard a noticeable click. She pulled up and removed the cap. Her heart was racing, it had been years since she had seen it, and it was the very thing that set her family up for the most epic journey she could ever imagine. With her right hand, she reached inside and pulled out a gold cylinder. On the side an inscription was etched above a seven-digit combination lock that read *Desired by all. Destined for one'*. She carefully turned each number to the desired code and opened it long ways. When her eyes feasted upon what was inside, she said, "How can something so beautiful be so deadly?"

ABOUT THE AUTHOR

John W. Vance is a former Marine and retired Intelligence Analyst with the CIA. When not writing he spends as much time as he can either with his family or in the water. He lives in complete bliss where the waves meet the shore

For more information on
John W. Vance
visit
www.jwvance.com
www.facebook.com/authorjohnwvance

If you have time please leave a review on Amazon.

Thank you,
John W. Vance

Additional book by John W. Vance

45092342R00141

Made in the USA
Lexington, KY
17 September 2015